GOOD FRIDAY'S CHILD AND THE GOOD FRIDAY AGREEMENT

Dr Brenda Josephine Liddy

Copyright © 2016 Dr Brenda Josephine Liddy
All rights reserved.

ISBN: 1537177052
ISBN 13: 9781537177052

My name is Patrick Sweeney.
I was born on Good Friday 1998. Sometimes I wonder if it was a good Friday. In Mark Twain's *Tom Sawyer* Huck remembers that it's Friday, an 'unlucky' day, and they put off treasure-hunting until later. Sometimes I wish I had been born on a Sunday because '… the child who is born on the Sabbath Day is bonny and blithe and good and gay'.

A funny thing happened today. Our English teacher was filling in our pink forms to enter us for the GCSE English examination and she exclaimed, 'Gosh, I had no idea most of you were born in 1998. Do you realise that you were born in the same year as the Good Friday Agreement? The revelation didn't cause much of a stir in the class. The teacher, Mrs Lundy, asked if we knew about the peace process in Northern Ireland that culminated in the signing of the Good Friday Agreement and if we understood its significance. A few mumbled something about having studied the Agreement in their history class, but most of the students just looked blank. Not to be bested, Mrs Lundy took it into her head there and then to set this as our discussion topic for our talking and listening practise. She told us that we were lucky not to have lived through the Troubles and not to have gone through those terrible years of killing and mayhem. Her words fell on deaf ears; all everyone wanted to do was to get the class over as quickly and painlessly as possible.

When I returned home that evening I picked up the *Belfast Telegraph* as Mrs Lundy had said we should read the paper every day because it tells us what is going on in the world and it would help us learn about the various types of articles journalists write. You'd think it was just words but, no, the words are doing things, important things. There are news articles and these are found at the beginning of the paper. They tell us about the big things that are happening in the world. Then there are feature articles, and these are more detailed and are usually about something topical. Then there are editorials, letters to the editor, columns and so forth. Mrs Lundy says it is very likely we will be asked to write a newspaper article in the exam. I hope we do as I don't like surprises. One year the task was to write a radio broadcast – that's pretty frightening. We also have to remember the 5 Ws: Who, What, Why, Where and When and GASP which means Genre, Audience, Purpose and Style.

I brought the *Belfast Telegraph* home with me the next night (it's free in the college), and I read the headlines: 'The Raining Champions'. There was an amazing picture of James Nesbitt, a famous actor from here, and one of Rory McIlroy, the most famous golfer in the world. Rory was sheltering under a black and white golf brolly with a NIKE logo printed on it and wearing a hat and fleece which were both emblazoned with the NIKE logo too.

There was also an interesting article in the paper about the welfare crisis at Stormont. Since Mrs Lundy had mentioned that we were going to focus on the peace process for our talking and listening I had decided to get a heads-up on its history. It was amazing that I was able to find out some information right away. I had thought I would have to do some online research on the Good

Friday Agreement, but I was surprised to find that the paper I lifted from college had an article which mentioned the political situation – it felt like Groundhog Day.

> But whether a series of new bodies envisaged in the December accord between the five Executive parties and the British and Irish governments ever get up and running remains in doubt, due to a destabilising Stormont wrangle over welfare reform. (28 May 2015)

I am not interested in politics but I am interested in language, and I noticed that there seemed to be a polarity of words in this sentence: 'accord' versus 'wrangle' – it seems a bit odd to have them both in the same sentence, and 'getting up and running' versus 'a destabilising Stormont' creates a weird contrast too. I have learned about paradoxical language and ambiguity in Shakespeare. After the witches had messed with Macbeth's head he lost his moral compass and declared, 'This supernatural soliciting | Cannot be ill, cannot be good'.

Anyone who knows me knows I like a challenge, and so I have decided I will carry out a full and thorough investigation of the Northern Ireland peace process – its background and inception, its implementation and its aftermath – and conclude whether or not it was a good thing to be born on the day the Good Friday Agreement was signed. Salman Rushdie's hero and narrator, Saleem Sinai, in his Booker Prize winning book, *Midnight's Children*, was born at midnight on 15 August 1947 in Doctor Narlikar's nursing home when 'clock-hands joined palms in respectful greeting'. Saleem tells us that he 'had been mysteriously handcuffed to history' and his 'destinies indissolubly chained' to those of his country. Nehru, the first Prime Minister of independent India, gave the following address to the Indian nation on the brink of midnight on the 14 August 1947, Independence Day:

At the stroke of the midnight hour, when the world sleeps, India will awake to life and freedom. A moment comes, which comes but rarely in history, when we step out from the old to the new, when an age ends, and when the soul of a nation, long suppressed, finds utterance.

I am the hero of this book, *Good Friday's Child*, and I was born on the very same day that Tony Blair stood on the steps of Stormont and delivered his famous eulogy:

A day like today is not a day for, sort of, sound bites, really – we can leave those at home – but I feel the hand of history upon our shoulders, I really do.

So while Tony stood on the steps of that historic building on that historic day, feeling the hand of history on the province, I, who a few moments ago was cocooned in a bath of amniotic fluid, was being handed to my mother after what the midwife termed a textbook birth – unlike the stormy birth pangs of the new Assembly. My mother's three terms were smoother than the three strands of the Agreement, which could be described as three straws with each party thinking that they'd drawn the shortest one. Their suspicions about each other led to each party believing that the other parties were pulling a fast one and leaving them no choice but to pull out of talks themselves. I was thinking of how apt the word 'strand' is as Belfast was built on a sandy ford across the River Farset. The word came from *Béal Feirste*, or the mouth of the Farset, which was an Irish word meaning 'sandbar'. As the poet Louis MacNeice wrote in *Valediction*, Belfast is built on reclaimed land.

If the strands were ever to be woven into a pretty plait like the ones you see on Goldilocks in fairy-tale books, both sides would have had to decommission more than their guns; they would have needed to decommission their ingrained versions of their own histories.

Winston Churchill was exasperated with the Irish Question. His outpouring of rhetoric during the war roused the people:

> We shall go on to the end, we shall fight in France, we shall fight on the seas and oceans, we shall fight with growing confidence and growing strength in the air, we shall defend our Island, whatever the cost may be, we shall fight on the beaches, we shall fight on the landing grounds, we shall fight in the fields and in the streets, we shall fight in the hills; we shall never surrender, and even if, which I do not for a moment believe, this Island or a large part of it were subjugated and starving, then our Empire beyond the seas, armed and guarded by the British Fleet, would carry on the struggle, until, in God's good time, the New World, with all its power and might, steps forth to the rescue and the liberation of the old.

But when it came to the Irish Question his rhetoric dried up like a grape in the sun. He said that the Great War had caused a huge upheaval where the world had been dramatically changed. Great empires were overturned, the map had been violently altered, hearts and minds had been transformed irrevocably. He had just returned from carving up Europe like you would a Christmas turkey: the big carve up of the Balkans was done in the blink of an eye with Russia agreeing to 90% control to Britain's 10%, and in Greece the formula was reversed whereas they went fifty-fifty over Yugoslavia. This was scribbled down on the back of an envelope and Joseph Stalin signed it like you would a cheque for goods. After the deal was done Winston Churchill hit a downer when he realised that as soon as the dust had settled he was not allowed to rest on his laurels:

But as the deluge subsides and the waters fall short, we see the dreary steeples of Fermanagh and Tyrone emerging once again. The integrity of their quarrel is one of the few institutions that has been unaltered in the cataclysm which has swept the world.

And after another half a century the waters were still falling short. The Agreement was beginning to look like a rag doll or a tattered remnant; a patchwork quilt where the quilters wanted to pull out the squares they didn't like. The ink had hardly dried on it and, of course, Jonathan Powell had forgotten to save the original on the computer. David Trimble wasn't happy with some of the annexes in the second strand ... the strand that would set the Orange bands on fire (some frightful images of intransigence crossed his mind).

Margaret Atwood wrote that 'War is what happens when language fails.' In respect of the Good Friday Agreement, peace happened when ambiguity prevailed. The Agreement could only work if the Nationalists saw a rabbit and the Unionists saw a duck. This image is often used in books on perception: if you look at the image one way, you see a duck and if you look at it another way, you see a rabbit. For example, this is from Article 1:

> The two Governments recognise the legitimacy of whatever choice is freely exercised by a majority of the people of Northern Ireland with regard to its status, whether they prefer to continue to support the Union with Great Britain or a sovereign united Ireland.

This is also from Article 1:

> The two Governments recognise that it is for the people of the island of Ireland alone, by agreement between the two parts respectively and without external impediment,

to exercise their right of self-determination on the basis of consent, freely and concurrently given, North and South, to bring about a united Ireland, if that is their wish, accepting that this right must be achieved and exercised with and subject to the agreement and consent of a majority of the people of Northern Ireland.

Does this mean that if the majority in the North wanted a united Ireland and the South of Ireland didn't, would that mean the country couldn't be united? The Unionists would settle for nothing less than duck à l'orange and the Nationalists wanted their rabbit made into Irish stew, so the only way the two sides could be satisfied was through a trick of linguistic ambiguity. As the parties climbed the stairs of Castle Buildings every day, Stormont's staircase became like Schroeder stairs where one side believed they were climbing upwards and the other side believed they were going downwards. This created frustration but it also saved the day – it was neither leading north nor south, but to ambiguity. Another trick of perception is the Young Girl–Old Woman Illusion, and just like that the Nationalists saw the Agreement as Cathleen ni Houlihan – the old woman who had four green fields, the four provinces of Ulster, Munster, Leinster and Connaught, that had been stolen from her. After requesting a blood sacrifice, three of her fields were returned to her … all except Ulster. The Unionists saw a young woman born in 1922, and this young woman wanted to keep her six counties intact and separate from the rest of Ireland. She was a legitimate lady and wouldn't dream of forsaking the blue skies of Ulster for the cloudy skies of the Irish Republic – a free state which had an allegiance to a foreign potentate in Rome, a free state which harboured and supported so-called freedom fighters who had affronted their young maiden and wreaked havoc on her people. As the deadline drew nearer the Nationalists saw the chance of delivering the fourth field to Cathleen ni Houlihan through constitutional means, and they focused on the words 'the people of the island of Ireland alone' while the Unionists concentrated on 'the legitimacy of whatever choice is freely exercised by a majority of the people of Northern Ireland'.

The second strand was about the Irish dimension, or North–South institutions. Now, cross-border cooperation sounded like a really hip idea in conflict mediation, but the reality for the Unionist party was that the border was not some airy-fairy concept but a fixed boundary making Ireland into two separate sovereign states. It was bad enough having Catholics in the North giving allegiance to a foreign pope, but to have the Taoiseach, his Dáil Éireann and Seanad Éireann (and who could even pronounce the word they used for their parliament – Oireachtas) having a say in Northern Irish affairs was too much.

Cross-border cooperation – who were they kidding? What fool's paradise did they come from? What planet did they live on? Ulster didn't want to share an electricity power line with them never mind share political authority. Would the meddling be mutual? Would Ulster politicians be permitted to attend Dáil meetings and make mischief? There was the distinct impression that a bunch of busybody blabbermouth bureaucrats had got together in a well-aired neutral venue with Ballygowan bottled water, palm plants and PalmPilots far away from the bullets, bombs and burnt out cars and hammered out a Belfast Agreement. Why is everybody afraid to say the emperor has no clothes instead of the emperor has a new suit? When the dealing was done, they came out on the steps of Stormont like a group of magicians and presented their agreement as if it was some kind of a fait accompli, as if they had performed a sleight of hand and produced the pièce de résistance, a masterpiece, a magnum opus.

John Dunlop, former Presbyterian Moderator, wrote, 'On a lovely summer's day, from some parts of the Antrim Coast Road, the coast of Scotland looks like a peninsula of Ireland. From that perspective, Dundalk seems a long way away, never mind Dublin and Cork.' He also stressed that, 'For very many Protestants, their contemporary East–West orientations are much stronger than any running North and South.' He pointed out that the divide is not only religious but also cultural: Irish people in the South read *The Irish Times*, for example, whereas in the North the Protestants read the *News Letter*. Most people in the South watch RTÉ and listen to Irish radio programmes whereas the Protestants in the North would prefer to watch the BBC and listen to Radio Ulster. Benedict Anderson wrote about how imagined communities are created through sharing culture and media:

> We know that [newspapers] ... will overwhelmingly be consumed ... only on this day, not that ... The significance of this mass ceremony – Hegel observed that newspapers serve modern man as a substitute for morning prayers – is paradoxical. It is performed in silent privacy ... Yet each communicant is well aware that the ceremony he performs is being replicated simultaneously by thousands (or millions) of others of whose existence he is confident, yet of whose identity he has not the slightest notion.

How was that going to go down on the Shankill Road? David Trimble knew they would have his guts for garters and his teeth for necklaces, they'd have his lungs for bellows, his blood for black pudding, his skin for lampshades and he could see his effigy adorning the Twelfth night bonfires. The Agreement was hanging on a thread, his career was hanging on a thread and his followers would hang him out to dry. He might agree, at a pinch, to the prisoners being released if they melted down their guns and rifles, but there was no way he could sanction a TD popping over the border to comment in Stormont like you would pop over to your folks on a Sunday for a cup of tea and a soda farl or advice on how to grow a hydrangea from a cutting. No, not even a wee maverick from the Shankill could endorse that. As he mused on his fate before the Agreement was a fait accompli, he could not get the image of Irene, the free spirit from the Shankill whom he had met at university, out of his head. Irene's father was a caretaker in the local Orange hall, and she went out of her way (or so her father claimed) to discomfit him at every opportunity. Once she had the audacity to bring her Roman Catholic friend to the house. Her father put his foot down and made it clear that he would have no Fenians in his house, and this remonstrance coupled with a knock to the head meant that Irene's cross-community efforts were dealt a fatal blow. Once she inveigled herself into the confessional at Clonard Monastery, but of course she didn't know the 'Bless me, Father, for I have sinned ...' spiel, so she was dismissed with 'Come back and talk to me when you have grown-up.' A poem by Rudyard Kipling kept popping into his head:

Kabul town's a blasted place,
    Blow the trumpet, draw the sword,
'Strewth I shan't forget 'is face
    Wet an' drippin' by the ford!

He supplanted Kabul with Belfast.

A rumour had come to him that morning that Jeffrey Donaldson was taking himself off on the pretext of a family holiday. David Trimble knew if he signed the Agreement, he would split the Unionist community, and he knew his tenure as First Minister would be turbulent but no doubt his golden handshake would be a peerage; Lord Trimble had a certain ring to it, he thought. Was this the decision Michael Collins was faced with when he signed the treaty which created the truce and paved the way for the Irish Civil War? Treaties and agreements – the way to hell is paved with good intentions! Imagine, he, the bastion of Unionism, had something in common with Michael Collins: both signed a document which brought an end to hostilities and both would pay the price. This might be the only thing he had in common with the big fella, Collin's moniker. Unlike Collins' father, Trimble's father was not the seventh son of a seventh son, and he didn't predict that his son would be a great leader. One of the treaty negotiators in 1921, Mr Birkenhead, when signing the treaty commented, 'Mr Collins, in signing this Treaty I'm signing my political death warrant' and Michael Collins said, 'I'm signing my actual death warrant.' David Trimble knew that he was committing political suicide. He could hear his detractors saying, 'Trimble sold us out. He sold us down the river.'

A Travel Brochure or the Cover of the Belfast Agreement?

Even before the document known as The Belfast Agreement arrived on everyone's doorstep, a technique known as false advertising was used to enhance its appeal. Of course the authors wanted the people to endorse the agreement and obviously a lot of thought went into designing the cover and make it more appealing to the point where the backdrop used came from another country, in fact another continent. Is the implication that the image of a Northern Irish dawn is not good enough to put on one of the most important documents ever to be drawn up in the journey to peace and reconciliation? In his *Irish Times* article, 'Picture of a perfect family not quite what it seemed', J. Mullin wrote that the image of the nuclear family looking out at a sunlit horizon on the front cover of the Agreement was not, in fact, an image of a Northern Irish coastline but was in Cape Town, South Africa. Both cities have suffered horrendous violence and are both are dealing with their horrible pasts. Could Belfast learn a lesson from Capetown's Truth Commission when it comes to sorting out the legacy of the past?

In his book, *The Moral Imagination: The Art and Soul of Building Peace*, John Paul Lederach, a world expert in theorising post-conflict societies, looks at where there has been a cycle of intractable violence. In his chapter entitled 'Peace Accords' he recommends that we 'explore the significance, promise and challenge posed by the image created by the word agreement'. He poses the question:

> What is the agreement? It is of course the signed document. But even the person in the street in settings of armed conflict will say, 'No, it is not the paper.'

He then comments that 'the prevailing image of agreement is the notion of solution', and he argues that an 'agreement creates the expectation that the conflict has ended'. He suggests that no one would be as frank as to say that 'the agreement represents processes for continuing the conflict under new definitions', but he urges communities in post-conflict situations not to be complacent. He argues convincingly that the peace accord is not a one-off event and left for the signatories to roll-out but is an ongoing process that involves the whole community. In a way the agreement is only a temporary scaffold which can be taken away when genuine dialogue and real cooperation take place. He warns us that the 'signed papers do not make a difference, and the agreements collapse unless the deeper processes of genuine engagement are created'.

Trying to forge a successful Agreement was like trying to catch a rabbit in a hole – once you thought you had the rabbit cornered, it was sure to have another bolthole, another escape route where it could get away. Maybe it was a metaphor for the rise and fall, life and death, beginning and end of all things, but every cycle needs a middle phase and the peace process didn't have any time to process or implement any of the recommendations, not even a dry run. If it was a garment, it went into the fast spin almost immediately and was then hung out to dry without actually having been washed. There was no saving the Agreement, and there was no safe haven. It kept going into cardiac arrest. Right away it was put to the test. It had no shelf life, it was mothballed, blackballed and so many were baying for blood. Whose Agreement is it anyway? No, all the spin in the world could make it wash, but not all the double-speak could make it wear.

'Read between the lines' and 'see the writing on the wall' – these were the phrases that were floating around David Trimble's head. And Tony Blair, that slippery eel was riding round like a unicyclist in a circus hoping to do a balancing act and shuffle back to Westminster after trying to shuffle off the Union like Shakespeare's mortal coil. And speaking of coils, the Sinn Féiners were like coiled springs all wound up and ready to bounce. David Trimble had heard that the British government had been communicating with Sinn Féin via backchannels, a series of unofficial negotiations, as Tony Blair wanted things sorted out in Ulster. Bertie Ahern and the Irish government were also conducting meetings with them, a sort of shadow diplomacy, as they also wanted a solution and an end to the Troubles. Bertie Ahern was unaware that Tony Blair was in secret talks with the republicans … it was a Johari Window. David Trimble had been at a presentation where this model was presented, and it was a perfect tool to explain the back channels, secret talks, talks about talks, talks behind closed doors and secret negotiations. David Trimble knew the British government were giving the republicans too much ground – virtually a licence to kill.

In the Johari Window model the first pane contains the things you know about yourself – this is also known as the Open Area. The talks could only work if there was transparency, but David Trimble saw that the pane was a little misted up sometimes and secret negotiations were taking place. This quadrant should have been where all the players were upfront and put their cards on the table; there should have been no double-dealing or secret bribes or assurances. The second pane is the Blind Area, which contains the things that other people know about you but that you don't know about yourself. David Trimble was aware that the Sinn Féin party saw themselves as liberators and not terrorists; they believed that they had the right to bring about a united Ireland through the bomb and the bullet, and now they were turning to the ballot box.

The third pane or quadrant was the Hidden Area. This was the one that the Sinn Féiners excelled in for they were the kings of subterfuge. Their intelligence was hard to breach and they operated their army on a nucleus of cells which were self-contained. It was a sort of no-win situation: the forces of the state couldn't wipe out the IRA as they were afforded protection within their own areas. The British Army and the police relied on a network of spies known as supergrasses, and this is how they gained information. A supergrass was an informer (or in local parlance, a tout) who gave evidence to the security forces in return for money and immunity from prosecution. There were the infamous supergrass trials which were scorned by both the IRA and the UVF. A lot of the convictions secured on the evidence were often overturned and the practice was eventually discontinued. The IRA could never defeat the security forces, and the UVF, UDA and IRA couldn't eliminate each other, so it was a catch-22 situation inside a conundrum wrapped up in an impasse.

The last pane was the Unknown Area in which no one knew the outcome. And who could have known the outcome? Senator Mitchell, Bill Clinton's special envoy, was hoping for a breakthrough, but the dreary steeples of Ulster were turning into deadly stakes which were striking at the heart of the Agreement. Jonathan Powell and the negotiating team stroked egos and settled tantrums but Ian Paisley was still stuck in his no-to-the-power-of-three mantra and he was out to deal the Agreement a fatal blow. He vowed to fight his corner on behalf of the Protestant people; he vowed that he wouldn't be backed into a corner, and his stance was obstreperous to say the least. David Trimble was not overly optimistic: everything had to go back to be rubber-stamped by the loyal brethren.

Meanwhile I of the flawless gestation and birth found that crying outside the womb was infinitely more effective than kicking my mother's womb. In fact, shouting in the womb was like shouting in space – no one ever heard you. So before I took my first steps or babbled my first 'Mama' or 'Papa', I gave full vent to my cries on every occasion that I felt a pang of hunger or felt that my mother ignored me for too long. My mother was so overcome with joy at the birth of her first baby that she was unaware of the significance of my birth being on the same day as the promising Agreement was signed. Some of the breaking news did filter through to the labour ward, but all the midwives and mothers were concerned about were breaking waters. My mother Alice was a graduate of the Winnicott school of child-rearing. She was all too aware of the primitive ego that was lurking beneath the surface of my beatific face. Maybe if she knew more about the Agreement, she would have described it as a curate's egg – good in some places and bad in others – but for now the Agreement was not her problem. Even though it was just the same age as her serene baby, Mother felt no obligation to fret about the new Assembly's frail ego. As Winnicott points out, the 'good-enough mother' begins as the absolute slave of her omnipotent child; his wishes are her command. The baby has total control of her attention; she gratifies his every wish; she indulges his every whim. Mother was aware that as a 'good-enough mother' she would give me a sense of control in terms of holding, handling and object-presenting. She understood the theory, but at times she felt that she couldn't completely satisfy my needs as I was always in need of something – food or comfort. She felt deeply connected to me, but at the same time she looked forward to implementing the second stage of Winnicott's theory: the transition stage, where my needs would be dethroned and I would no longer have my needs completely satisfied on my terms. Maybe I wasn't king after all!

This was the stage where I would have to learn that Mother is not on this earth to fulfil my needs continuously. This readjustment was where I would learn that life is a series of winning and losing, getting attention and being ignored; I was understanding failure. To adhere to Winnicott's schema, a teddy was produced as a transition object for me. And in accordance with his schema, I was given total control over it – to love, cuddle or tear it to pieces. This transitional object would be central to my life until I became disenchanted with it and it would be thrown in the skip.

So my home life continued happily for the first few years. Mother was convinced that my physical and psychological development was going according to plan, or at least according to Winnicott's plan. She had heard horror stories about cot death or sudden infant death syndrome, but after the first six months she was less apprehensive. I was responding to the schema and becoming an integrated whole being on account of the fact that my mother, like a finely tuned piano, had hit all the right notes in creating a stable holding environment, and when I was handed teddy my transition from 'absolute dependence' to 'relative independence' was assured. There were a few false notes along the way, a few bum steers, a few bumpy rides, but overall she felt that she was getting to grips with her new role as a 'good-enough mother'. She had heard that some mothers were capable of holding their infants and some were not – not just physically holding but creating a psychological space as well. And my mother had to be a holder, otherwise I would have cried incessantly and felt insecure. Yes, she was more than a 'good-enough mother', she was a perfect mother. I was bathed in her maternal love and her powerful ego strengthened my fragile one. She protected me from physiological insult and injury and had gone out of her way to turn my room into a child-friendly cocoon which was not too hot, not too cold but just right, like baby bear's porridge. She ensured that my surroundings were calm and melodious, that I never experienced loud music or aggressive voices. She made sure that my room was decorated with pastel shades which would help me to feel calm and collected. She wouldn't be like Virginia Woolf's mother who was cruel and distant to her talented daughter – if it was not for the colourful flowers on the wallpaper, poor Virginia would have been even more deprived of sensory stimuli. She was delighted with her success in preventing me relapsing into some kind of primitive agony where my defence mechanisms would cause me to revert to my 'unintegrated state' – I would never die a cot death or a Winnicott death! She documented my every sneeze, every cough and every rash as if she were being filmed, and if she had have been filmed, the child psychologist would have seen a mother who was creating a safe holding environment for her son similar to an airplane being held in a holding pattern waiting for permission to land. A baby cannot possibly land on the runway of life – he has no language, no tools. Mother was so finely attuned to me that she would take my feelings and verbalise them: 'You're a tired wee baby, aren't you? You're a hungry baby … Oh baby's feet are a little cold … Oh, baby, that noise scared you!'

I had these feelings of falling off the world and nothing seemed concrete. I needed Mother to chew reality for me and then, by a series of cooing and baby talk, she let me know that I wasn't falling into infinite darkness.

My first six months under the auspices of my mother's watchful eye were backed with Winnicott's theories of holding and not dropping. We coexisted in this calm cocoon, and she synchronised her walking to my breathing when she carried me about the kitchen. She listened to my very heartbeat, breath and even my pulse. I was just this bundle of flesh and bones that had been shoved into an alien world of air and gravity after leaving her oceanic womb. Now she had to take over the instinctual role of the placenta, the umbilical cord and the amniotic sac whereas when I was in her womb all I had to do was absorb the nutrients and vitamins that streamed in via my navel. I had lived inside a little balloon in her stomach, and it was she who had to face the maternity hospital and negotiate the birth. From my birth she knew that if she made a sudden bolt or a jerky movement, I would feel the discord, and her actions emulated Winnicott's paradigm of the to-and-fro bond which he argued was the basic building block of nurturance. This was made possible through Mother's previous experiences of working in childcare, and of course she had been a baby once herself (and to all accounts a very contented little baby). But for me this was my first experience of being a baby, and I had no prior experience to draw upon. Sometimes when she was rocking me she sang me a song:

> Hush-a-bye baby
> On the tree top,
> When the wind blows
> The cradle will rock.
> When the bough breaks,
> The cradle will fall,
> And down will fall baby
> Cradle and all.

While my mother was going to-and-fro and tiptoeing around me, Jonathan Powell was going to-and-fro among the panes in the Johari Window hoping for a breakthrough. He felt that all this grandstanding, last-minute deal-making, eleventh-hour reprieve was somehow synonymous with the Irish psyche. In the Unionist camp there seemed to be raised voices behind the locked doors. The Sinn Féin camp were purring like Cheshire cats and loved to receive the occasional pat on the back from America or Dublin or indeed from any part of the globe. It was important to them to convey an aura of taking the moral high ground by giving up the armed struggle, one of their cherished ambitions, and they were acting like coming to the negotiating table was almost a holy grail too far. They were getting hell from their rank-and-file volunteers, many of whom had served time in 'the Kesh', who felt that they were being short-changed. What could Gerry Adams do to keep the diehards at bay, those whose mantra was Charles Stewart Parnell's war cry that 'No man has the right to fix the boundary to the march of a nation'? Jonathan Powell even admired Adam's gall in keeping the talks on track and not losing his temper. Yes, the psyches of the Unionists and Sinn Féin had been moulded in the crucible of history.

I imagined that Jonathan Powell had grown to hate Castle Buildings and dreaded stepping out of the helicopter like some kind of deus ex machina dropping in to save the talks. What was being sold to these politicians was more like snake oil. He must have thought it was like a kind of window dressing and not the real deal. He would have had visions of the Band-Aid not sticking for too long. Powell was aware of how these deals panned out; he knew that if they signed their Good Friday Agreement, it would be plain sailing for a while and then it would all be up in the air. As soon as those blades started rotating and they took off across the Channel tongues would start wagging and heads would start rolling. Not much wonder Tony Blair was so jittery. If India's memory had undergone what Rushdie terms as chutnification, the memories here were dipped in formaldehyde – Damien Hirst could add to his shark exhibit and dip this province in formaldehyde. Yes, just take the folk on the hill and dip them in formaldehyde, and Castle Buildings as well. Jonathan Powell said, 'From the very day I set foot in it, I felt I was being chloroformed, rendered hazy with sick building syndrome.' I couldn't believe the state of the place, its Formica panelling was in a poor state of repair. Couldn't they spend some money on it and get it spruced up? The whole place was a warren of corridors and it was impossible to get your bearings. Not much wonder the place was in a tumult. It must have been one of the longest political stalemates in history. And it wasn't as if they'd never had a good prime minister.

The Formica was being chipped away gradually and civil rights were being chipped away zealously, and now the building had become ill and the community had fallen apart.

The building reminded Jonathan Powell of the lines from Shelley's elegy to Keats:

> And grey walls moulder round, on which dull Time
> Feeds, like slow fire upon a hoary brand;

Ironically the setbacks and the stalemates, the standoffs, the deadlocks and the grandstanding unleashed Powell's creativity and one could imagine him writing a mock soliloquy about the situation which he crafted from Richard III's famous speech at the opening of the play *Richard III*:

> Now are the ripples of discontent
> Made gloriously smooth by
> This PM of England
> And all the qualms that
> Lingered in the Castle Buildings
> Deep into the dungeon buried
> Now are our grudges hung up
> For museum artefacts,
> Our swords turned into
> Ploughshares, our crosswords
> Turned to cross-community
> Dialogue. Our contentious
> Parades to agreed determinations
> The grim face of war

> Now shines with an inner glow
> And now instead on planting
> Deadly bombs to blast
> The limbs of innocent people
> And killers going hell-for-leather
> On tit-for-tat
> Rampages, Ulster
> Will be a halcyon of peace
> And not a war zone.
> We will have to accept this
> Warped document, forged
> In Dublin and London
> Half of it made up, to brow
> Beat us into submission.
> It cannot be entertained.
> We will hatch a plan
> to counteract this popish plot
> We will not be shut up or shut out
> By those treacherous ones
> We will not capitulate
> These capers will have to stop.

Sometimes random similes would pop into Jonathan Powell's head:

> The agreement was looking like a beached whale
> And Tony was running up and down with buckets of water
> trying to revive it.

It is fashionable in modern literary theory to speak of the collapse of the great narratives in favour of a more subjective interpretation of the world. In his book, *The Postmodern Condition*, Jean-Fran ois Lyotard wrote that the postmodern condition was moving towards a plurality in what Wittgenstein termed as language games.

Barthes wrote that 'language ... ceaselessly calls into questions its origins'. He argued that the author is like a God producing an infallible, foolproof text, but that a text emanates from a multi-dimensional space where a diverse number of meanings mingle and collide. Point in case: not all Catholics are nationalists, not all nationalists are republicans, not all republicans support an armed struggle, not all republicans want to abandon the Armalite rifle for the ballot box – for some it's *Tiocfaidh ár Lá* not *Tiocfaidh* Armani in a six-counties state. On the other hand, not all Unionists support the UDA or hate hurling or the Irish language. There was a line of graffiti on the wall near the Westlink, at the bottom of the Falls Road, which said, 'Níl mé do steiréitíopa' which means, 'I am not your stereotype'.

In terms of religion they live in parallel worlds, even though they both profess to be Christians. For example, regarding the doctrine of transubstantiation, or change of substance, Catholics believe that at the consecration of the Mass, when the priest changes the bread into the body of Christ and the wine into the blood of Christ, it becomes the real body and blood of Christ. Protestants do not believe in the doctrine of transubstantiation, but many of them partake of Communion. What do they believe Communion to mean if they do not believe they are receiving the body and blood of Christ? Both religious groups read the Bible, and this following passage from the Gospel of Mark refers to the last occasion in which Christ shared a meal with his apostles:

> And whilst they were eating, Jesus took bread; and blessing, broke, and gave to them, and said: Take ye. This is my body. And having taken the chalice, giving thanks, he gave it to them. And they all drank of it. And he said to them: This is my blood of the New Testament, which shall be shed for many.

And yet Protestants do not believe in the real presence of Christ in the sacrament, and that the eating of the bread and the drinking of the wine are done to remember Christ – 'Do this in remembrance of Me'.

It all boils down to semantics!

In using ambiguous language in the Agreement document, the authors were not only drawing on postmodern theories of the plurality of meanings and the collapse of an unequivocal meaning or interpretation of words and text, but they were unconsciously drawing on a classical precedent. In his book, *Athenian Constitution*, Aristotle argues that in order to harmonise inter-group conflict he deliberately used ambiguous phraseology, thereby allowing laws to be passed without a hitch, and, in so doing, was able to strengthen the role of the 'demos' – the ordinary people.

The proof of the pudding is in the eating!

The Agreement negotiators used a more Lewis Carroll approach to the wording of the Agreement document:

> 'The question is,' said Alice, 'whether you can make words mean so many different things.'
> 'The question is,' said Humpty Dumpty, 'which is to be master — that's all.'
> Alice was too much puzzled to say anything; so after a minute Humpty Dumpty began again. 'They've a temper, some of them — particularly verbs: they're the proudest — adjectives you can do anything with, but not verbs — however, I can manage the whole lot of them! Impenetrability! That's what I say!'

With the two sides wanting to be master, it was tough to reach a consensus, so the draftsmen used the same cunning as Humpty Dumpty did with Alice – every time he used a word like impenetrability, he made it do a lot of work and he paid a bit extra for it.

> 'Would you tell me please,' said Alice, 'what that means?'
> 'Now you talk like a reasonable child,' said Humpty Dumpty, looking very much pleased. 'I meant by "impenetrability" that we've had enough of that subject, and it would be just as well if you'd mention what you mean to do next, as I suppose you don't mean to stop here all the rest of your life.'
> 'That's a great deal to make one word mean,' Alice said in a thoughtful tone.
> 'When I make a word do a lot of work like that,' said Humpty Dumpty, 'I always pay it extra.'

Like Humpty Dumpty on the narrow wall, who at any moment could accidently fall, the Agreement could fall apart at any moment and all the prime minister's horses and all the Taoiseach's men would struggle to put it together again. So a compromise had to be reached, and the words had to work hard enough to save the deal and ultimately to spare lives. Strand One, the one that would strengthen the umbilical cord with England, was the one that was going to be a thorn in the republicans' flesh. Their Schroeder staircase was heading down south, whereas the Unionists' one was heading to Westminster. And Dublin's staircase was going to have to be rejigged:

> The Irish Government will introduce and support in the Oireachtas a Bill to amend the Constitution as described in paragraph 2 of the section 'Constitutional Issues' and in Annex B, as follows: (a) to amend Articles 2 and 3 as described in paragraph 8.1 in Annex B above and (b) to amend Article 29 to permit the Government to ratify the new British–Irish Agreement.

The Agreement was premised on the auxiliary verb 'may', and as to paraphrase Humpty Dumpty, the negotiators owed it a fortune. An auxiliary verb is a verb used in forming the tenses, moods and voices of other verbs. The primary auxiliary verbs in English are be, do and have, and the modal auxiliaries are can, could, may, might, must, shall, should, will and would. So to get rid of the artillery they had to use auxiliaries! After Strand One had been hammered out, the thorn in the side of the Nationalists became the thorn in the crown of the Unionists, so in went the modal auxiliary cavalry. The North–South Strand of the Agreement was indebted to the modal auxiliary:

> Areas for North–South co-operation and implementation may include the following:
> Agriculture – animal and plant health.
> Education – teacher qualifications and exchanges.
> Transport – strategic transport planning.
> Environment – environmental protection, pollution, water quality, and waste management.
> Waterways – inland waterways.
> Social Security/Social Welfare – entitlements of cross-border workers and fraud control.
> Tourism – promotion, marketing, research, and product development.
> Relevant EU Programmes such as SPPR, INTERREG, Leader II and their successors.
> Inland fisheries.
> Aquaculture and marine matters.
> Health – accident and emergency services and other related cross-border issues.
> Urban and rural development.
> Others to be considered by the shadow North/South Council.

Meanwhile, my mother was hoping to return to work in her childcare job at Little Gems Nursery, which was situated in the local university.

One day, her mother, Grace, commented, 'Patrick is very quiet.'

'What do you mean?' inquired Mother. It was strange that her mother, whom she loved above anyone in the world, could suddenly manifest as a two-headed gorgon – whoever said that a new baby unites the wider family? My mother felt the opposite. She wanted to tell her mother that I was just a contented little baby, and why should I be otherwise considering her years of experience in looking after children, not to mention her immersion in Winnicottian schemata? Grace persisted and said, 'He doesn't babble. And he doesn't seem to watch you when you're picking him up. To put it mildly, your baby doesn't wear a happy expression. And when you speak or coo to him, he doesn't seem to respond. Yet he seems to react when there's the sound of a dog barking outside.'

'Oh, Mum, I think you're being overly dramatic. He's just a bit sensitive. Are you sure you're not looking to find fault with him because I don't have the same time to spend with you any more?'

'Oh, Alice, I have to admit that I was a little lonely when you went into your baby bubble – it was as if you were the only two people on the planet. But I have adjusted – I go to the flower-arranging class in the college, and I have made some new friends.'

My mother was more concerned about my next challenge. She was lucky enough to have secured a place for me in her nursery, and on the allotted day I was strapped into the car and off we headed. It felt strange being strapped into the back of the car; it made me feel trapped. I don't like my freedom being restricted like this; it's all part of controlling children.

It was September and the students had returned. It was more of a commuter university and the campus life was not particularly lively. Some students rented accommodation in Portrush and Portstewart, and, needless to say, the freshers were enjoying getting blocked and partying for the first few weeks.

When my mother arrived at the nursery she noticed that the wall displays were exactly the same as they were six months ago. The wall for the Mr. Men and the Little Miss characters were as follows:

Mr. Brave, Mr. Busy, Mr. Chatterbox, Mr. Cheerful, Mr. Clumsy, Mr. Dizzy, Mr. Funny, Mr. Fussy, Mr. Grumble, Mr. Grumpy, Mr. Happy, Mr. Impossible, Mr. Jelly, Mr. Lazy, Mr. Messy, Mr. Mischief, Mr. Miserable, Mr. Nonsense, Mr. Nosey, Mr. Perfect, Mr. Quiet, Mr. Right, Mr. Silly, Mr. Skinny, Mr. Slow, Mr. Small, Mr. Sneeze, Mr. Snow, Mr. Tall, Mr. Tickle, Mr. Topsy-Turvy, Mr. Uppity, Mr. Worry, Mr. Smiley, Mr. Good, Mr. Rude, Mr. Cheeky, Mr. Christmas, Little Miss Bossy, Little Miss Brainy, Little Miss Busy, Little Miss Chatterbox, Little Miss Contrary, Little Miss Curious, Little Miss Dotty, Little Miss Fickle, Little Miss Fun, Little Miss Giggles, Little Miss Greedy, Little Miss Helpful, Little Miss Greedy, Little Miss Late, Little Miss Lucky, Little Miss Magic, Little Miss Naughty, Little Miss Neat, Little Miss Quick, Little Miss Scatterbrain, Little Miss Shy, Little Miss Somersault, Little Miss Splendid, Little Miss Star, Little Miss Stubborn, Little Miss Sunshine, Little Miss Tidy, Little Miss Tiny, Little Miss Trouble, Little Miss Twins, Little Miss Wise.

She noticed that Little Miss Sunshine was drooping a bit, so she made a mental note to pin her up when she got a free moment. Little Miss Giggles' colour was fading and needed to be repainted and Mr Christmas was out of season. It was hard to believe that the manager, Miss Watts, could let the wall display get so dilapidated; her idea of a stimulating play area was a sandpit and a few nursery rhymes stuck on the wall. She had a preference for tongue twisters:

Betty Botter bought some butter
But she said this butter's bitter
If I put it in my batter
It will make my batter bitter,
But a bit of better butter
Will surely make my batter better.

So she bought a bit of butter
Better than her bitter butter
And she put it in her batter
And her batter was not bitter.
So t'was better Betty Botter
Bought a bit of better butter.

She also liked Humpty Dumpty:

Humpty Dumpty sat on a wall.
Humpty Dumpty had a great fall.
All the king's horses and all the king's men
Couldn't put Humpty together again.

When my mother brought me into the nursery, all the other nursery workers gathered round to welcome her back. While she enjoyed basking in all the good wishes, she noticed that I was putting my hands up to my ears as if to block out the noise. My mother resumed her duties in the nursery but it wasn't long until Miss Watts called her into her office.

'Patrick doesn't seem to be settling in. Have you noticed that he seems to be quiet? He's not making any eye contact with Catriona, and he won't respond to any visual stimuli.' It was amazing how one minute all her colleagues were swarming around her like locusts to compliment her on her new baby and the next they had turned into a nest of hornets zapping her with negativity. Everybody had suddenly become an expert on my behaviour. No one gave babies a chance anymore; if they aren't babbling and cooing, there's something wrong with them, and if they are babbling too much, then they have some kind of hyperactivity disorder.

My mother wished she didn't work in a nursery – suddenly there was too much scrutiny. She wished she had stayed off for another few months because maybe I would have had a better chance to become more responsive. Now it was too late. In the space of a morning her manager and her colleagues had more or less labelled me as autistic. All these Mr. Men characters were up on the wall but the only one a baby was allowed to be was Mr. Perfect. What about Mr. Slow, Mr. Small?

> Miss Watts arranged to carry out an assessment on me the following day. It was a test based on the research of Collis and Schaffer where mother and baby are brought into a room with brightly coloured toys. Ideally the baby would focus on one of the toys and become fascinated by it. The mother, responding to the baby's interest in the toy, would then focus on the same toy and mention some characteristic about it in order to establish a rapport with him. My mother waited for me to show an interest in one of the brightly coloured teddy bears, but I just gazed ahead as if I were in some kind of trance. She felt like lifting the big blue teddy and dancing round the room making funny faces. I could almost imagine her doing the tarantella like Nora in Ibsen's *A Doll's House*. But, unlike Nora, she knew the dance, the dance of baby care. She couldn't believe it. What had happened to me, she wondered. She had followed Winnicott's 'good-enough mothering' regime religiously, but obviously the regime didn't factor in autism. Obviously autism has a mind of its own and doesn't subscribe to any methodology, Winnicottian or otherwise. And, unfortunately, you cannot assume that Winnicott is like

Woolworths where one size fits all. She was an advocate of his theories before my birth, but now she had her doubts. I must admit you could learn a lot about my mother from reading her diary. She seemed to rely a lot on Winnicott, and then she moved onto Kübler-Ross. She appeared to have no real thoughts or ideas of her own. As the weeks rolled by and we digested our new configuration of autistic baby and mother of autistic baby, the Agreement was running out of steam. Ciaran Carson sees the infrastructure of the road as a metaphor for backward thinking:

For if time is a road, it's fraught with ramps and dog-legs, switchbacks and spaghetti; here and there, the dual carriageway becomes a one-track, backward mind.

(*Belfast Confetti*, pp.27-28)

Someone commented that Northern Ireland's motorways were bite-sized Mars bars. For example, you could join the M2 at Nelson Street, and, if you were heading from Belfast to Coleraine, a town fifty miles away, you would experience what a bite-sized Mars bar's road infrastructure would look like. After leaving the M2 at Junction 1 you would take the A26 exit and then you would proceed on to the Lisnevenagh Road, after that you would drive on to the A36, and this is where it gets surreal, for at Kilraughts Road roundabout you drive onto Frosses Road. There have been many fatal accidents on this infamous stretch of road. As Wesley Johnston, a road enthusiast, has asked, 'Why does a 4.5 mile stretch of the M2 lie in splendid isolation, detached from the rest of the M2 to the south? The answer is, as it always is, that grander things were planned. The M2 was originally planned to go from Belfast to Coleraine.'

The piecemeal progress of building a motorway from Belfast to Coleraine reflected the stops and starts of the implementation. On 11 February 1998, Northern Ireland's devolved government was suspended. It was as if the people and the politicians were unable to stay on the highway to government and felt the need to take to the byways instead. One of the biggest stumbling blocks for Trimble and the Unionists was that decommissioning hadn't started and the bullet was still on the table with the ballot box.

On paper the M2 from Belfast was a great idea, but it never happened. Who was to blame? The planners, the Troubles, the economy, a myriad of excuses. On paper the Good Friday Agreement, a sixty-five-page document, which by some miracle was signed at the eleventh hour by the main stakeholders, looked good. It was a model of compromise and diplomacy, and the negotiators were as euphoric as Candy was in Steinbeck's *Of Mice and Men* when he heard about George and Lennie's American dream to buy a little farm. Lennie and George hatched a scheme where Lennie would have a rabbit hutch and George would have a cabbage patch, but Crooks had seen men planning to live off the fat of the land before. He said that many of the migrant workers fantasised about getting a piece of land but 'Nobody never gets to heaven, and nobody ever gets no land.' The best-laid plans of mice and men are often thwarted. The negotiators honed the draft with care and precision over many months in the hope of getting to a 'yes' diplomacy so that both sides could accept the unacceptable. Accolades poured in from all over the world. The buzzwords boomed on all the airwaves. Words like 'jumping together', 'choreography' and 'mood music' filled the hopeful air.

The negotiators were like chefs in a resort where all the diners had to agree on a set menu except only half the diners liked fish and the other half demanded meat. How to get an agreed menu? And for this to work it couldn't have been all duck or no dinner, so a shared dish had to be agreed on. For example, prawn cocktail for starters and lamb stew for the main course. Northern Ireland's

Titanic crashed into an iceberg on its maiden voyage, DeLorean's car factory hit the skids, but the Agreement would flourish.

The doors of the DeLorean car opened upwards and they looked like a seagull's wings. In France they are known as *portes papillon* – butterfly doors. The car was a metaphor for the city reaching up to the sky, climbing up above the bombs, the bullets and the burnt out cars. Icarus, whose wings were built to sustain him on his journey, didn't heed Daedalus' warning not to fly too close to the water in case the salt water would dampen the feathers and not to fly too close to the sun because his wings would melt but to follow the correct flight path. Instead of taking care and flying at a midway point in the sky, he soared too close to the sun, his wings melted and he plunged to his death. Daedalus was a famous Greek master craftsman who built the labyrinth on Crete in order to confine the Minotaur, a creature that was half bull and half man. King Minos became enraged with Daedalus because he revealed the secrets of the labyrinth to Ariadne who in turn disclosed them to Theseus who made his way in and killed the Minotaur. King Minos punished Daedalus by imprisoning him and his son Icarus in the labyrinth. Daedalus designed wings for himself and his son so that they could escape from their prison.

Like Icarus, seagulls love to glide and drift along the shore riding the current and have no fear of the salt water or the sun or any of the elements, nor do they need to. It's the same as indulgent parents who buy their son or daughter a sports car and say 'Don't drive too fast.' All children are like Icarus, they want to test their wings and push the boundaries. As Oscar Wilde, an admirer of Icarus, wrote:

> Never regret thy fall | O Icarus of the fearless flight | For the greatest tragedy of them all | Is never to feel the burning light.

The negotiators who crafted the Agreement were like Daedalus who fashioned the Labyrinth on Crete – although it was a masterpiece it proved almost impossible to navigate. You want a labyrinth to be a path, not an impenetrable maze.

I cannot get the image of Icarus, the seagull, the car with the butterfly's wings out of my mind. How we were all gullible voting for the Agreement, thinking it was a silver bullet, a miracle cure, but it turned out to be a quick fix, a sticking plaster. I found this poem about a seagull by Herbert Bashford.

The Seagull

A ceaseless rover, waif of many climes,
He scorns the tempest, greets the lifting sun
With wings that fling the light and sinks at times
To ride in triumph where the tall waves run.

The rocks tide-worn, the high cliff brown and bare
And crags of bleak, strange shores he rests upon;
He floats above, a moment hangs in air
Clean-etched against the broad, gold breast of dawn.

Bold hunter of the deep! Of thy swift flights
What of them all brings keenest joy to thee—
To drive sharp pinions through storm-beaten nights,
Or shriek amid black hollows of the sea?

Although the Agreement didn't crash on its first outing; it seemed there wasn't enough lifeboats for the three strands of the document. And while it didn't claim to be the greatest sports car in the world or to be unsinkable, it was too modest for that, it didn't fare much better than either the *Titanic* or DeLorean. It made no grandiose claims – it was a treaty of hope, a roadmap for peace, although Seamus Mallon commented that is was 'Sunningdale for slow learners'. The latter was on the table in 1973, however its first few steps were tentative. The euphoria ran out of oomph and the rhetoric was running on empty. Hammering out the Agreement was like *The Myth of Sisyphus* – when the rock was finally at the top of the hill, it rolled back down again. Establishing normal rule in Ulster was like the twelve labours of Hercules: carrots got the horses to water but the horses didn't want to drink; stick would have to be applied. The Agreement didn't hit an iceberg and sink to the bottom of the ocean it just capsized from time to time. When things got rocky, the plug was pulled, the Assembly was suspended and direct rule was restored. The captains had to take their hands off the rudder and wait until the storm subsided. This went on for a few years: some carrot, some stick, more promises and more compromises, more horse-trading and more Hillsborough summits.

You were no longer frisked going into shops and there were no more killings, but roadblocks and dog-leg switchbacks appeared. Phrases like 'an armed peace' were heard, and it looked as if the ship would sink and the car would crash after all. Like the path of true love the path to peace is not smooth. Treaties are not worth the paper they're written on or the ink expended on them if the people don't sign up to them. The people of Northern Ireland were used to the dynamic of war: the warmongers, the security forces and the long-suffering public. But, ironically, the suicide rate was low and the paramilitaries kept the drug dealers under control, usually with beatings or kneecappings.

This peace was a fiction, a fabrication. The people had not developed the tools to hoe the peace. Eighty walls were dotted about the interfaces, and one had the dubious distinction of being among the highest in Europe. Pieces of the biggest wall in Europe, the Berlin Wall, were now exhibits in museums, but this province wasn't ready for this kind of museumisation. Believe it or not, peace is hard work because it means giving up something in order to achieve a better society. In war you have a role, a *raison d'être*, and peace building is more challenging than that.

There's a comedy sitcom set in Belfast called *Give My Head Peace* which satirises paramilitary groups and local politics. It's a healthy part of the peace process when a community permits themselves to be ridiculed, and although Ulster people may have some deficits in their characters, a lack of humour isn't one of them. In fact, it has been said that they possess a gallows humour which can be a great advantage. 'Give my head peace' is an Ulster colloquial saying for please don't annoy me with your silly behaviour. It seems that Ulster people are good at asking for headspace and not so good at making room for shared space.

The Agreement seemed destined to share the same fate as *Titanic*, one of the most majestic ships in the world. The engineers, the draughtsmen, the riveters, the fitters, the turners and the boiler makers were proud of its lavish restaurant, its Turkish baths, its electric lifts and its squash courts – not one rivet was missing! The Agreement was like that: a work of art, the politicians' *pièce de résistance*, their best group endeavour.

The negotiators, like crafty Daedaloi, had worked their cunning and brought this document to perfection. It would be a vehicle to lift the province out of the doldrums. If there was enough goodwill it could be a game changer. Artifice is all very nice and rhetoric can win over hearts and minds, however the proof of the pudding is in the eating – when the handshakes are over, when the champagne is popped and everyone gets a slap on the back, when the photographs are taken and the ink on the signatures has dried and the honeymoon is over, when Bertie Ahern has gone back to Dublin, Tony Blair to No. 10 and George Mitchell to America. Mitchell was buoyant. Blair was ecstatic; he had grabbed history by the throat and hadn't let it go until he had the answer he wanted. Ahern was bowled over. The parties had reminded him of Goldilocks in the fairy tale of *The Three Bears*: the porridge was either too hot or too cold, the chairs were never right – they were either too wide or too big, the beds were never right – they were either too hard or too soft. Finally Goldilocks got the right porridge, the right chair and the right bed. And finally these characters had made a porridge that most of the parties could eat, a chair that most of them could sit on and a bed that most of them could lie on. Ian Paisley, of course, wasn't into the fairy-tale ending, and he wanted to change the happily ever after to they all fell out and it ended in tears. He was furious at this devil's pact and wished a plague on all their houses! These Mephistophelian dealings would perish as sure as the snowflakes would melt in the thaw. He wouldn't sup with the Devil or have dialogue with a backward, priest-ridden Republic.

> Harden not your heart, as at Meribah, as in the day of Massah in the wilderness.

For a few short weeks the sun shone on the Agreement and there was a sense of euphoria, but after a few sunsets a post-Agreement depression set in. The Agreement sprinted down the big hill at Stormont bursting with pride, boasting to everyone that it was all over bar the shouting, it was a done deal. The Agreement had been given a sound medical and seemed robust. Yes, it seemed to be roadworthy but it still hadn't been road tested. It seemed fit for purpose, a breakthrough, a quantum leap, yet there was still some trouble ahead. That final sprint became a power-walk, and then it was a dawdle, and, in the end, it collapsed in a heap.

It had been pushed through on a wing and a prayer, a last-ditch effort. The Ulster people waited with bated breath for the long-sought-after peace. The result of the referendum was a huge boost for the Agreement. Not only was it signed by parties who didn't see eye to eye (more an eye for an eye and a tooth for a tooth), but it was ratified by the majority of the electorate who were elated at the prospect of peace.

The protagonists, the new MLAs-in-waiting, carried the Agreement down from the house on the hill as proud as Punch and, like Moses in the Old Testament, presented their pact to the people. Every time Moses turned his back the people murmured that they wanted another miracle otherwise they would smelt down some gold and erect a golden calf because they didn't like all the hitches and glitches. So it was with the Agreement; there was enough trust to build it but not enough faith to implement it. Everyone was fed up with the affliction of the Troubles and it was peace at any price, even a compromise, even an appeasement, though neither could say they were like peas in a pod or that Taigs could be Prods – no way, not by a long chalk. The Israelites were prepared to follow Moses blindly, to get away from Rameses and the Pyramids and the beatings, but once they were in the desert it was a different story. They got fed up meandering and eating the same old manna every morning for what seemed like ages, and they began to murmur and make trouble. Similarly, the groundswell of goodwill created by the Agreement soon abated.

The Unionist camp was growing edgy. David Trimble was having a meltdown over the decommissioning dithering: the guns weren't being melted down as had been promised. What was to be done? The Agreement was only words, and no matter how laced it was with compromises and promises, how gorged with guarantees, it was only words and words were not deeds. There is a saying, 'Don't follow a man's words but follow his feet.'

Living Like Protestants
It isn't the people's fault that they are slow to learn their lessons from the history of the conflict. Captain Terence O'Neill, who was prime minister of Northern Ireland, tried to explain his views to

the Protestant people, but he might as well have talked to the hand because the face wasn't listening:

> It is frightfully hard to explain to Protestants that if you give Roman Catholics a good job and a good house they will live like Protestants because they will see neighbours with cars and television sets; they will refuse to have 18 children.

He went on to say:

> But if a Roman Catholic is jobless, and lives in the most ghastly hovel, he will rear 18 children on National Assistance. If you treat Roman Catholics with due consideration and kindness, they will live like Protestants in spite of the authoritative nature of their Church.

Captain Terence O'Neill became prime minister in 1963, following Lord Brookeborough. He may have been another one of Banquo's descendants succeeding a previous Banquo, but to say this would be a grave injustice to the man. Not only did he have the same name as the famous O'Neill clan, but his father died in action in WWI and his grandfather, Lord Crewe, was in favour of Home Rule. O'Neill was not cut out to perpetuate a Protestant State for a Protestant People. He had fought in WWII, and was shot and captured for a brief spell in Holland. This was the man who had tea with Emperor Haile Selassie, entertained the troops with his French ditties during enemy bombardment and spared the life of a Mongolian prisoner. This was the man who visited Catholic schools and then invited Seán Lemass, the Irish Taoiseach, to Stormont for talks in 1965. This was the man who then crept off to Dublin for further meetings with Lemass and no doubt the notion of a United Ireland was discussed. O'Neill was ready to bury the hatchet and saw the value of cross-border cooperation over economic issues. Lemass was prepared to butter up the North by exempting it from Britain's quota on butter imports. But it was not to be. More lessons were needed to be learned before the slate could be swept clean. Lemass and O'Neill saw eye-to-eye and both men were prepared to extend the hand of friendship. But their eye-to-eye caused O'Neill's party to go head-to-head with him and the new mantra was 'O'Neill must go'.

O'Neill had tea with the Queen, but the notion of abolition of the border was not to be brooked by Her Majesty. Ulster constraint was not to be tempered by a Celtic freedom. He commented that 'While good men sleep, and honest men play golf and bridge, the unwavering ones are zealously chipping away at the principles of democracy.' This is similar to a saying of Edmund Burke: 'All that is necessary for evil to succeed is for good men to do nothing.'

The meetings between O'Neill and Lemass were discontinued as the Unionists felt a cold chill blowing through the corridors and while they could see that the heat was turned up again to keep their dynasty cosy at all costs, it was, at the same time, to freeze out any notion of more Belfast–Dublin stuff. In describing the civil war in Algeria, Camus used the metaphor of a forced marriage to describe the two sides:

> It is as if two insane people, crazed with wrath, had decided to turn into a fatal embrace, the forced marriage from which they cannot free themselves. Forced to live together and incapable of uniting, they decide at last to die together.

The Agreement was the only way to prevent the kiss of death to the marriage.

> If you took the six counties, you could
> Have a state-of-the-art exhibit for the
> Museum of Stuckism.
> Damien Hirst would have a field day.

> And all the Agreements concessions,
> Covenants which were
> Reputed to be solutions, are merely
> Compromises, quick fixes
>
> Going round and round
> In circles like Johnny the
> Horse in Joyce's story 'The Dead'
> Who plodded round and round
> King Billy's statue as the
> Treadmill routine was so ingrained.

There is a song about a famous roundabout called 'Mickey Marley's Roundabout'. It was written by Seamus Robinson, a Belfast man, in 1976:

> Mickey Marley had a wee horse –
> Kept it at the back of the house of course.
> It wouldn't eat grass and it wouldn't eat hay –
> But it would eat sugar lumps all the day.
>
> Mickey got some wood and wheels for a start –
> And then he sat down and made a wee cart.
> He hammered and he hammered and he footered about –
> Until he'd built a Roundabout.
>
> (chorus)
> Round and round and up and down,
> Through the streets of Belfast town –
> All the children laugh and shout,
> Here comes Mickey's Roundabout.

Good Friday's Child and the Good Friday Agreement

Mickey Marley was born in the Markets area of the city, and for forty years his hobby-horse roundabout toured the streets with children paying a penny for a ride. The politicians were like Mickey Marley, touring around the little streets, but although people showed interest at the beginning they soon got off the horse and refused to get on again.

As Belfast was built on reclaimed land, like Louis MacNeice said in *Valediction*, maybe the foundation of the city was too shaky for anything to take root. Matthew wrote in the Gospel that the person who listens to God's word builds his house on solid rock, and even though the storms lash it, the floodwater rises and it is battered by rain, it will not fall because it's built on the bedrock.

> Ciaran Carson writes, 'And the streets are a bad photostat grey; the ink comes off on your hand | With so many foldings and unfoldings, whole segments of the map have fallen off.' Agreements are written in ink and the ink was starting to fade.
>
> (*Belfast Confetti*, pp.27-28)

Keep A Diary and One Day it Will Keep You
Monday, 14 September 1998

Dear Diary,
I hated my first day in the nursery. All those nursery rhymes and Mr. Men and Little Miss characters displayed on the wall – and all those babbling infants! They were so noisy. They had absolutely no idea that I am a gifted baby. And I don't want to play their stupid games. I'm not saying I'm Rain Man or anything, but the moment I was born I had the reading age of a Cambridge professor. I'm not saying that I could hack into Nasa computers, but I could pretty much do basic programming from the first time I used my mother's laptop. They call it savant syndrome or splinters skills or, even more poetical, islets of ability. In my case I have an exceptional ability to read (also known as hyperlexia). Obviously I won't get a library card at my age, and therefore my access to books has been curtailed, so for the last five months I have been restricted to my mother's choice of books, which happens to be the *Belfast Telegraph* and child psychology books by Winnicott and Klein. I have played along with her Winnicottian schema for the first months of my life, but that has only been possible because I'm in that small living room with her most of the time and things follow a similar routine every day. The only time my routine changes is when my nanny, her mother, comes to babysit me while my mother goes out to shop. I pretend to be sleeping when my nanny's there because she's a very silly woman and she watches the most mind-numbing daytime TV. I cannot believe that anyone actually enjoys Jeremy Kyle. Lines like:

> These guys have lost their way.
> He gets around.
> I'll prove your fiancé stole twenty pounds from my children's holiday money.

> My husband is dressing like a woman, but is he sleeping with men?
> He's old enough to be your grandfather.
> I'll prove I had your husband's baby.

make me worry about the state of the world. There's no satisfying Nanny's hunger for tabloid talk shows, but at least my mother likes watching David Attenborough's wildlife shows which are great.

I was just about keeping it all together when my mother plonked me into my baby seat in the car and whizzed me off to her place of work, which I was shortly to learn was my place of suffering. All I saw, apart from those ridiculous posters on the wall, was other babies who I took an instant dislike to. As Sun Tzu said, 'No battle plan survives the first contact with the enemy', and Little Gems was full of enemies. How could I consider the feelings of other babies whom I had never met before? I had no blueprint, no socioscheme to rely on. And as for imaginative play, well I might as well just rule that out now – I would rather search for UFOs.

After the test was over I envisioned a battery of other tests and a lifetime of interventions; my mother was a paid-up member of the intervention school of diagnostics, treatments and interventions. There was another baby who had been put on a programme for autistic children, and just by dint of good fortune I was able to go on the same programme after my preliminary screening. The programme was called the SCERTS model, which stands for Social Communication, Emotional Regulation and Transactional Support. While I was digesting this information like a savant sponge, my mother seemed to need a handkerchief because her eyes were watering. I have seen her needing to dry them before after phone calls she made to someone who owes her money. Apparently someone from the Child Support Agency is trying to chase up a man who should be paying for my food and my clothes. I don't like these phone calls, but I do like the taste of one of the formula milk brands that my mother is feeding me. Over the last few weeks she has been offering me foods which have felt very mushy on my tongue, so I spat them out – but not in an aggressive way. However, after a few types had been proffered and subsequently rejected by me, I found one that is quite palatable. I like the Cow & Gate My First Bolognese, or maybe it was just the sauce. Then, for dessert, I discovered the Hipp Apple & Pear Pudding was also quite tasty.

Back Channels
Sometimes meetings took place in an airport hotel and nothing was written down, not like a meeting where there is an agenda. The most significant meeting which led to the ceasefire and brought about the Good Friday Agreement was held in a hotel near Heathrow. The MI5 man went by a different name to give the meetings a secretive aura, and this time it was Fred. The IRA also used multiple identities – one of which was Kevin, a shorthand for, 'I don't know your brief or how much leverage you have, but I am from the IRA and I have one brief which is scribbled on this note: the war is over.' That the war was over seemed to be clear, but Fred was adamant that this must not be construed as an act of surrender. And MI5 couldn't bring a speaking note because in this sort of meeting there are no rules and no agenda; it cannot be a case of brinkmanship or one-upmanship. They say the first casualty of war is truth, well the first casualty of peace talks is transparency. Sometimes Fred couldn't wait to get out the door. He was used to this hush-hush, back of envelope, cloak-and-dagger stuff, but Kevin took it to a new level. The MI5 man had a secret admiration for the volunteer. What could he possibly be getting out of this? He was part of an organisation where you finished up dead or in prison. Although his own life was pretty abnormal, at least MI5 looked after you and you were doing something for your country which was mandated by the government. It wasn't like a James Bond film where your cigarette lighter could be a flamethrower, a

dicky bow could be a camera, a Rolex wristwatch could contain a laser-beam cutting tool and your fountain pen could fire an explosive charge. They didn't give you a fake fingerprint, a pocket snap trap, Japanese prosthetics, a bowler hat which could cut through stone or a garrotte watch. No, there wasn't even an Austin Martin or a 'shaken not stirred' Martini cocktail. It was all about recruiting agents these days, or operatives as they were known, and it was them that took the real risks. He could never really tell anyone what his daytime job was, so he had to curtail his social life, and of course he was lonely at times, especially during covert operations. But he still felt he had more going for him that this volunteer whose hair looked as if he had done a bad job dyeing it himself. However, Fred thought, you've got to hand it to the IRA. They can still recruit enough volunteers to keep their army going. He wondered what made this man live a life on the run, without home comforts, always looking over his shoulder, watching his back, following orders, dealing with informers, carrying out 'jobs'.

In regard to giving, the Bible advocates that the right hand shouldn't know what the left hand is doing, and this not knowing what Tony Blair was conceding to Martin McGuinness or what guarantees David Trimble was assured was the glue that stuck the Agreement together. There was only so much Gerry Adams could cede without backing down or giving up on the republican ideal of a united Ireland, and no doubt the Army Council wouldn't be happy with a sell-out after thirty years of a costly armed campaign. If they were letting go of their cherished dream of the end of British rule in the North, they needed some compensation, and this came in the form of pardons for a number of on-the-run volunteers. The wind had certainly shook their barley, but they weren't going to melt down one single gun until they had an early release scheme for the prisoners who were serving their sentences in the Maze Prison. The secret of a happy marriage is compromise, and forced marriages are rarely happy unions. Making an honest woman out of the Agreement was not going to be a walk in the park. These concessions were not made or agreed on in an open and honest manner. Instead, what was told in secret would some day be shouted from the rooftops. Indeed, it would all come out in the wash!

And sometimes it seemed like Hobson's choice: either accept this or you will get nothing at all. This was the only show in town.

The Curse of Macha
Is Ulster cursed? There is a legend that a pre-Christian woman called Macha was forced to compete in a race while heavily pregnant with twins after her husband Cruinniuc boasted to King Conchobor of her racing prowess. Fleet of foot, and despite her condition, she outran the King's horses. After winning the race she gave birth to twins, and the name Armagh means the twins of Macha. It is said that she put a curse on Ulster men that when they went to battle they would experience labour pains and become ineffective. When Queen Maeve attacked Ulster in order to get possession of the brown bull of Cooley, the curse fell on the Ulster men and they were unable to fight, all except Cuchullain who eventually defeated her.

They say the way to hell is paved with good intentions, and sometimes it must have felt that the highway to peace was more like the road to hell.

Ulster could make the greatest ship in the world and inspire one of the greatest movie makers to make one of the greatest movies in the world based on it. *Titanic*, directed by James Cameron, was the first film to gross over two billion dollars worldwide. Ulster was also the birthplace of the most innovative sports car in the world – the DeLorean which appeared in the film *Back to the Future*.

> Marty McFly: Wait a minute, Doc. Ah ... Are you telling me that you built a time machine ... out of a DeLorean?

From a humble street in the east of the city the greatest footballer in the world could be brought up and an airport named after him. George Best recalled how he had been dating Miss World and took her the races. They won £5,000 and went back to their hotel where they started counting the money on the bed and a waiter arrived to bring them champagne.

Belfast could produce the greatest snooker player in world, Alex Higgins, who had a snooker hall named after him.

> 'Listen, nobody's as fast as me, nobody's as attractive as me to watch. I'm the Cassius Clay of snooker.'

And with these illustrious precedents it was not hard to believe that Ulster could produce the greatest Agreement in the world, and so the world waited with bated breath.

Where did it all go wrong?

To Collaborate or Not
They'd rather clobber each other than collaborate! It's like sharing a space with your worst enemy. Can you build a vision when your promised land is a thirty-two county Irish Republic and an end to the border, and the other side's vision is for the union with Britain to be maintained lock, stock and border? The modal auxiliaries in the Agreement would have to do somersaults, backflips and every contortionist's bend in the book so as not to go belly-up. The commas were straining, the full stops were complaining, public confidence was waxing and waning and was then back on track again!

> Chalk and cheese.
> Flip-chart marker and feta cheese.

The British had pulled out all the stops, David Trimble was blowing his top, the Shinners were saying, 'We're on top' and everyone was saying top and tail it or top it up.

Game on, game on, gone game and ball in play again. Send the garment back for more alterations: it's a straitjacket, it's too strait-laced, too restricted, we can't live with this. Our pips are squeaking; they're forcing us into a Procrustean bed and our legs are like stumps – we cannot stump out any more.

The ball's in their court. Keep your eye on the ball. No matter how many tucks and darts you put in this dress, it will never be ready for the big day. It will always have an ugly-sister feel to it. It's like trying to make a silk purse out of a sow's ear.

This is neither fish nor fowl, neither rank and file, nor fully fledged anything!

What the hell, do they think we're wet behind the ears? Do they think we came down the Lagan in a bubble or came down in the last shower? No way, Jose! We know what side our bread is buttered on and we know what foot we dig with.

Nobody was giving much away literally or metaphorically. When the Indians were signing a treaty with the white man they laughed at the idea of signing away the land. How can you possibly sign over land? How can you possibly own land?

Everyone felt short-changed, out of pocket. David Trimble banged the Agreement down on Senator Mitchell's desk and said he had drawn the short straw. He would have to withdraw; the other side were getting too many concessions. The DUP said the North/South Council was the straw that broke the camel's back. Tony Blair was like a drowning man clutching at straws. Gerry Adams argued that you can't make bricks without straw and that every brick would build a new house in which they would have a place and it would no longer be a cold house for Catholics. Bertie Ahern could see by the straws blowing down south what way the winds were going and he preferred Sunningdale; it would have given the Irish government a chance to meet with their northern counterparts, but that wasn't in the new Agreement. In a way, it was an Agreement brokered for the Falls and the Shankill, not for Belfast and Dublin, and so the Taoiseach's input was curtailed.

I must admit I wasn't as anxious this morning, although I didn't sleep very well. I suppose I'll get used to the crèche, but I still dislike the other baby buggies arriving with all those boisterous babies hanging out of them and their mothers dashing off in their upmarket cars to their professional jobs. Their time is so precious yet they couldn't wait to have their little bundles of joy.

It must be hard for a mother to cope with a child who has a disability. I only have her to look after me, and I don't want to go into care as you hear about how they treat you in those homes. And I couldn't bear to be touched by anyone never mind be fostered by them and have to move into a strange house which could have annoying children. It has taken quite a while to convince my mother that I will never eat cauliflower or any vegetable with florets, and I would prefer not to have to start from scratch again explaining my special dietary requirements. It's just too awful to contemplate. Autists' ethics are different.

What We Resist Persists: Some Reflections on the Ghosts of Agreements Past and Not
Necessarily in Chronological Order

The various parties working in their various offices in Castle Buildings were like the ghosts of former agreements: the Sunningdale Agreement which tried to set up a power-sharing Northern Ireland Executive and a Council of Ireland on 9 December 1973, and the Anglo-Irish Agreement which was signed on 15 November 1985. It seemed as if the agreements were destined to endless revisions, repackaging and reiterations. The protagonists in 1973 were Brian Faulkner, the last prime minister of

Northern Ireland; William Whitelaw, the Secretary of State; John Hume, the SDLP leader; Edward Heath, the British prime minister; and Liam Cosgrove, the Irish Taoiseach. Brian Faulkner was triumphant as he believed that the principle of consent was assured and that Northern Ireland's status as part of the UK was copper-fastened, but the Irish Taoiseach was marketing it as a stepping stone to a united Ireland. Meanwhile Hume was burning the midnight oil and keeping the pressure on Heath to secure the best deal for his party.

Was it a step too far, too much too soon, too little too late? Was Dublin just a Sunningdale away? Was it a vehicle to drive the Unionists into a united Ireland? Was it a bridge too far? Were there too many sacred cows, too many Arks of the Covenant? Meanwhile the IRA was stepping up its campaign of violence, and Paisley was getting geared up to destroy the Trojan Horse. The only people who praised Sunningdale were the signatories themselves, and the moment the architects flew back from the civil service college in the Royal County of Berkshire all hell broke loose. The Ulster Workers' Council strike commenced, and instead of power-sharing the power was switched off and the province was plunged into darkness. Northern Ireland was brought to a standstill and the way was paved for another decade of violence and mayhem. But not all the bridges were burnt and new ideas would spring from the ashes. Although Sunningdale got a bum's rush, its ghosts would meet again to re-enact another bunfight, another muffin-worry, and another agreement would be forged from the detritus. More blood would be shed and more limbs would be mangled, more buildings would be flattened and more cars would be burnt out, more candles would be lit, but in the end more ink would be spilt and more midnight oil would be burned as the ghosts gathered round for another séance.

The atmosphere must have been electric in Sunningdale. Isn't it astonishing that the leaders from three cities could stay in the one room for three days and get on so well – especially as they were all coming from different standpoints? Dublin wanted to have a say, the Unionists were saying hands off, the British were saying we'll find a way just get it sorted and the SDLP were holding sway – after all it was their day, their brainchild.

The Clashing Rocks and Ambiguous Bridges
I'm interested in how the ambiguous language used in the Agreement built a bridge which led to its signing and subsequent implementation. After carrying out some research I realised that I had to go back to Sunningdale and to the Anglo-Irish Agreement.

When the negotiators returned to their cities they must have each felt like Jason bringing home a Golden Fleece. The only thing was that too many people felt fleeced rather than recompensed. As they sat in that building in Berkshire they must have felt that they had conquered the raging bulls of hatred and sailed their Agreement through the Symplegades, the huge rocks that Jason had to navigate his passage through in order to obtain his holy grail. The people, like the Harpies, desecrated the sacred fleece.

The negotiators faded like Banquo at the feast in *Macbeth*, disappearing like worm casts, and the little tunnels of hope were flattened.

Sitting there in peaceful Sunningdale they must have felt like they were heart surgeons performing a complex heart transplant, and surely they took great care in the operating theatre. The Agreement would give Ulster a brand new heart, and, if things went according to plan, the new heart would help life get back to normal: the troops would go back to England, the parcel bombs would stop, you wouldn't have to check under your car for devices or keep your head down, there would be no security checks, no more surveillance, no more dawn raids, no more bombs or bomb scares, no more controlled explosions or intimidations, threats or beatings, no more doors being kicked in or heads being kicked in, no more kneecapping or phone tapping or petrol bombing, no snipers, strikes or three-minute warnings to evacuate a building, no more marches, no more supergrasses or supergrass trials or Diplock courts and not recognising the court, no more touts, no more lookouts, no more bin-lid banging, no more duck patrols or army searches, no more arms caches or men on the run or tit for tat or bookies and pubs being sprayed with bullets and helicopters whipping up the callous sky with their blades. A rising tide lifts all boats, but a hovering helicopter sinks all hearts – no more foreboding! Ulster must have felt like some kind of unwilling conscript in a dodgy experiment, or some kind of freak being studied by rather erudite doctors who had decided to make it more compatible with normal life. The operation went excellently and no doubt the heart would function well and blood would pulsate through the body red and rejuvenated. But, unfortunately, the eminent surgeons hadn't noticed the patient's weak immune system. This *deus ex machina* was a catastrophe.

They say writers should have a chip of ice in their hearts, and it may have looked as if the Sunningdale scribes were deliberately sinking the boot into the Unionists. The naysayers buoyed themselves for a fight. They would have preferred to have been a Protestant majority in a six-county statelet than a minority in a thirty-two county Ireland. Their fears were understandable – who doesn't want to protect their interests?

Each time an agreement was forged one side saw it as a solution but the other side saw it as a sell-out. The aftershock of Sunningdale was felt for weeks. It was as if the corner counties had been shaken with an earthquake followed by a tsunami. The Unionists couldn't connect with the new status quo: any interference from Dublin seemed like a bridge too far. They had had a good innings and there was every chance they could continue to enjoy rich pickings – it was just a matter of getting their batting team assembled and out onto the pitch again. A sticky wicket wasn't the end of the world, and overall their batting average would ensure that they would get into the game again. A corridor of uncertainty had been created by those with an axe to grind, but they had no idea what they were up against. The Unionists wouldn't allow the ink to dry on that document. It would be charred beyond recognition and its naïve proposals to establish a power-sharing executive and a North/South Council quashed. They would see that the stepping stones out of Ulster's political impasse as laid down by the Agreement would become stumbling blocks to its implementation.

Thatcher's Treachery
Some people in the Protestant community were enraged by the Anglo-Irish Agreement; it gave the Republic of Ireland a say in Northern Ireland's affairs and they saw it as weakening the union between Ulster and Great Britain. Arthur Aughey explains:

> Since 1969 Unionism has been on the defensive ... There has developed the impression that Unionists have lost control over their own destiny. Many Unionists feel that their position is being bartered away in secret deals between the British and Irish governments.

The Anglo-Irish Agreement brought new players onto the chessboard. The Treaty, as it was known, was signed in 1985 and created a framework which enabled both countries to form a government together. The new role given to the Republic of Ireland in Northern Ireland's politics and the promise of cross-border cooperation triggered a series of protests.

Even if tissue types are closely matched, transplanted organs, unlike transfused blood, are usually rejected unless measures are taken to prevent rejection. Rejection results from an attack by the recipient's immune system on the transplanted organ. It can be mild and easily controlled or severe, resulting in the destruction of the transplanted organ which the body regards as foreign and battles to discard.

Peter Barry, Irish Minister for Foreign Affairs; Tánaiste Dick Spring; Taoiseach Garret FitzGerald; British Prime Minister Margaret Thatcher; Geoffrey Howe, British Minister for Foreign Affairs; and Tom King, Secretary of State for Northern Ireland, were all at the signing of the Anglo-Irish Agreement. Margaret sat there like the queen bee in a hive of worker bees, albeit a press-ganged queen bee because she admitted privately that 'if this meant making limited political concession to the South, much as I disliked this kind of bargaining, I had to contemplate it'. Her middle-class middle-of-the road elegance was expressed in her black jacket with its classic brooch and a tailored skirt, her white and red blouse with its pussycat bow, her pearl earrings and her coiffed hair. Her clothes were sourced from Marks & Spencer or Aquascutum, a store that once made coats for the Crimean War. She considered the latter a reliable heritage brand, and she respected the advice of Kingsley Matheson Pink, her dresser at the flagship store in Regent Street.

Seamus Heaney said that, 'Everybody in the north is born with a sense of solidarity with one or other group ... So the emergent self grows up carrying responsibility of the group – holding the line, keeping up the side.'

Padraig O'Malley said, 'Language is central to the lack of understanding between Roman Catholics and Protestants. Nationalist leaders talk about "frameworks" while unionists prefer to deal with definite proposals.' He added that, 'Both the Anglo-Irish Agreement and the Downing Street Declaration were written in a language which Protestants could not understand. They were devised to allow for latitude – and that's what Protestants can't deal with.'

The Downing Street Declaration was another attempt to bring peace to the province. It was a joint manifesto between John Major, the British prime minister, and Albert Reynolds, the Irish Taoiseach, and was the result of a series of secret meetings and negotiations. It was signed on 15 December 1993, and it stated that the Irish people had the right to self-determination on the basis of consent and that if the majority wished it, a united Ireland could be brought about. The Declaration paved the way for the Good Friday Agreement. It was obvious that the stakes had been raised in the poker game and many Unionists felt that the link with the United Kingdom was being undermined and the road to Dublin was being paved.

John Waters, an Irish Times journalist, wrote, 'As in poker it is not necessary to have substance on your side, so long as the illusion of substance can be maintained in language.'

Sinn Féin's Gerry Adams said the buzzword was 'alienation'. Margaret Thatcher didn't like that word as she thought it too Marxist.

A new word entered the lexicon-the totality of relationships in these islands.

In public Margaret Thatcher was intransigent, but she was holding meetings behind the scenes. Garret FitzGerald commented that:

'I had come to the conclusion that I must now give priority to heading off the growth of support for the IRA in Northern Ireland by seeking a new understanding with the British Government, even at the expense of my cherished, but for the time being at least clearly unachievable, objective of seeking a solution through negotiations with the Unionists.'

Garret FitzGerald sported a wire-wool hairstyle and wore a contrite smile – more nutty professor than Machiavellian statesman – and he spoke at a rapid speed. But he did know how to appeal to her number one priority: security – that was the carrot that drew her in.

She called him Gareth as Garret stuck in her throat.

Ian Paisley was like a man possessed. He led massive rallies against the Anglo-Irish Agreement. The phenomenal attendance at these anti-Agreement demonstrations has been well-documented. Over 100,000 people gathered in Belfast to hear anti-Agreement speeches from James Molyneaux, leader of the Ulster Unionist Party, and Ian Paisley, leader of the Democratic Unionist Party.

Ken Maginnis said that Margaret Thatcher, the embodiment of Conservatism, had betrayed them. The writers, the negotiators and the draughtsmen of the Agreements were like tenacious authors with baggy manuscripts trailing around thousands of publishers looking for a publishing deal.

Serious and Solemn Agreement?
The two communities in the North were like the Khalkotauroi: a pair of fire-breathing bulls with bronze hooves and bronze mouths who were virtually impossible to yoke together. Bigger men than Garret FitzGerald had tried and failed. Ireland didn't have its Jason yet.

Charles Haughey brought her a teapot and she accepted it. She said he hoodwinked her with his Irish charm and blarney.

Garret FitzGerald brought Hillsborough and heartache. She felt beaten by her own handbag which she thought was her hand grenade. Her hairdo, which survived the Brighton bomb, was wilting. Her 'watershield', her Aquascutum, was compromised. She had brought her handbag and her wish list which included helicopter overflights into the South and extradition.

If Sunningdale was a short-lived sticking plaster, then the Anglo-Irish Agreement was an out-and-out disaster.

Margaret Thatcher said: 'If we get back next time,' (referring to the general election in 1983) 'I think I would like to do something about Ireland.'

There was no ladder of progress that the politicians could climb and lead the province to the promised land of peace and progress; no miracle cure could be found.

The Agreement was foisted on the Unionists, and therefore the new organ was rejected at once. From the moment Maggie Thatcher arrived in Hillsborough Castle their backs were up, the Union Jacks went up and the assurances which should have acted as immunosuppressants acted like freeloading germs.

In the Bible, in the territory of Jezreel, the dogs shall eat the flesh of Jezebel. Ian Paisley called Margaret Thatcher a Jezebel; the Iron Lady had become the painted lady. She had sold them out, sold them down the river, sold their birthright. She was the iron hand in the velvet glove, and the song he sang to her was a 'Song of Faith Forsworn' by Lord De Tabley. Two of the verses are below:

> Take back your gifts.
> False is the hand that gave them; and the mind
> That planned them, as a hawk spread in the wind
> To poise and snatch the trembling mouse below.
> To ruin where it dares—and then to go.
> Take back your gifts.
>
> Take back your words.
> What is your love? Leaves on a woodland plain,
> Where some are running and where some remain:
> What is your faith? Straws on a mountain height,
> Dancing like demons on Walpurgis night.
> Take back your words.

Margaret Thatcher, who declared that Ulster was as British as Finchley, her constituency in the south of England, was going to have to revise her opinions. She'd always claimed she was English to the marrow, but once she reluctantly admitted to Sir David Goodall that her great-great-grandmother was Irish and that made her one-sixteenth Irish.

The Unionists' tempers flared up and on the day of the first intergovernmental meeting they were not going to mince their words or bandy them about. They were like Banquo who was unable to attend Macbeth's inauguration feast because he had been slain. The Unionists had been left out in the cold but they were not going to go quietly. Macbeth alters the mood round the table by hallucinating and imagining that he sees an apparition of Banquo at the table. Lady Macbeth tries to save the situation and declares:

> You have displaced the mirth, broke the good meeting,
> With most admired disorder.
>
> Macbeth

Ian Paisley and Harold McCusker, the deputy leader of the Ulster Unionist Party, and their camp followers displaced the mirth and sent a strongly worded letter of protest to the Secretary of State, Tom King, who was chairing the inaugural meeting:

> In the name of the Unionist majority, whose rights you have trampled in the gutter, we repudiate you. The sordid exercise in which you are involved is the very antithesis of democracy. Today you debase yourself to the level of an equal with the imposter Barry – the lowest form of political existence – who has no jurisdiction in this realm and who, parasite that he is, has been carried to your table on the back of the murdering IRA [Irish Republican Army].

Hyperbole is an extreme form of expression. As Du Marsais puts it:

> We use words which, taken literally, go beyond the truth and represent the most or the least order to convey some

excess up or down. Our hearers discount from our words what needs to be discounted.

It was ironic that the Anglo-Irish Agreement, which was supposed to bring the two communities closer together, only succeeded in driving them further apart.

The Khalkotauroi bronze bulls were digging their bronze hooves in even deeper and the fire that emanated from their bronze mouths was even fiercer. The words of protest from Ian Paisley and Harold McCusker were like a barrage of poison arrows that punctured the surface of the Agreement and sank it like a lead balloon. Tom King would have needed more than a magical potion to protect him from the toxicity.

Dear Diary

Dear Diary,
I'm glad it's Wednesday and we're halfway through the working week because my mother looks exhausted. She spends her days with two year olds, and while I know they're called the 'terrible twos', she has twelve of them to look after. They're all 'normal' as far as I know. One child is called Ben, and I don't think I've ever witnessed such antics – he pulled a toy from another little boy and wouldn't give it back. I think my mother is a saint for putting up with them. She looks after them all day and arranges so many wonderful activities for them. Their mothers look stressed out by the time they come back for them, and although they make a fuss over their progeny initially and ask their little princess or prince what kind of a day they had and say things like, 'Tell Mummy what you did today?' and 'Did you tell Alice about your new toy?' and so forth, you just know they're glad their children are tired out and will go to bed and sleep and give their heads peace.

De Bono is a famous expert in creative thinking. He developed a parallel thinking model; a tool that helped a person or a group be more innovative and productive. The group is given the opportunity to use parallel thinking and thereby generate a new perspective on given topics using different coloured hats: blue, red, yellow, green, white and black. He envisaged groups starting with the blue hat, which is used to set out the aims and objectives of the meeting. The group would then put on the red hat to garner the feelings and opinions of the group; the emotions and intuitions. The next hat is yellow and it is used to gather the positive and constructive elements of the situation. During the green hat session the group would be asked to generate creative and resourceful ideas. The white hat session would involve fact finding and is concerned with only facts. It's like a white computer screen: you just put the facts in and it stays completely neutral. Finally, the black hat session would engender possible downsides and challenges; it plays devil's advocate.

The six hats was not a methodology that anyone had thought of using in the Good Friday Agreement negotiations, but some of the key players acted like they were wearing De Bono's hats.

As the notorious headmaster Thomas Gradgrind from Dickens's *Hard Times* commented:

> Now, what I want is, Facts. Teach these boys and girls nothing but Facts. Facts alone are wanted in life. Plant nothing else, and root out everything else. You can only form the minds of reasoning animals upon Facts: nothing else will ever be of any service to them. This is the principle on which I bring up my own children, and this is the principle on which I bring up these children. Stick to Facts, sir!

Sir Ken Bloomfield, wearing the white hat, pointed out that the facts were hidden from the Unionists and he felt the negotiations were one-sided:

> I would wish it to be clear that I share the view expressed by a number of colleagues that the Agreement as drafted is fundamentally flawed, by reason of its ambiguity, its one-sidedness, and above all the grave risk that it will serve to destabilise rather than to stabilise the situation in Northern Ireland.

He also commented that although the Irish government was communicating closely with John Hume and the SDLP, 'the British Government accepted no matching obligation to keep unionist parties in touch'.

It was interesting to read the opinions expressed in the Seanad Éireann on 27 November 1985 (the Seanad is the upper house of the Irish Parliament). Wearing a red hat Senator Andy O'Brien said 'that Seanad Éireann welcomes the Hillsborough Agreement and calls on all persons of goodwill to work for the success of this initiative in the interests of peace and stability in Ireland'. The speaker went on to enumerate the heinous deeds committed in the North, and he said, 'A knock on the door or window pane can indicate that violent death is only seconds away from a father or son of the household.' The Taoiseach did acknowledge that the Unionists 'were understandably concerned about the secret nature of the lengthy negotiations'. He also commented that 'Although it was necessary that they should be secret, it was perhaps unfortunate that they were so long.'

Tom King, Secretary of State for Northern Ireland, wore a black hat when he expressed concerns that the Agreement was giving too much to the Irish side. In a secret memo to Thatcher he expressed the following:

> I have to say, with some reluctance … that the agreement as it stands strikes me as offering considerably more to the Irish than it does to us.
> It will certainly be so perceived by the unionists. The imbalance seems to me to lie in the following: the Irish are being given an unprecedented foothold in the internal affairs of a part of the United Kingdom.

He concluded by saying that 'If these points can be met, I still believe it right to seek an agreement; but the balance of advantage is a fine one.'

Mr Lanigan pointed out the pitfalls inherent in the Agreement and how it legitimised partition:

> We will never sacrifice the entire basis of constitutional nationalism on the altar of an agreement which breaches

sovereignty and legitimises partition and the British presence in Ireland.

The yellow hat calls for looking at the positive aspects in a proposal. The Irish Taoiseach, Garret FitzGerald, wore this hat. He created the groundwork that paved the way for the Good Friday Agreement. He created a consensus at a time when there was a strained relationship between Ireland and Britain. Added to that, the Unionists boycotted the talks and Sinn Féin wasn't permitted to attend because of its endorsement of the IRA. And to add fuel to the fire Margaret Thatcher had nearly been killed by the IRA after they had bombed the Grand Hotel in Brighton where she had been staying during the Tory Party conference. Apparently her hair withstood the trauma of the blast and she thanked her hairdresser personally for giving her a bombproof hairdo. Her hair was redone by her personal crimper a few days later, but her sense of outrage was not so easily fixed. In the end Garret FitzGerald used a mixture of Irish charm and Prospect Theory to negotiate with the British Prime Minister. Garret FitzGerald's contention that the Irish government had the right to have a consultative role in Northern Ireland's affairs was initially abhorrent to her, but, finally, she was persuaded to accept the Taoiseach's proposal, and in return the Irish government had to agree that the North's constitution couldn't be changed without the majority agreeing to it. In other words, there couldn't be a united Ireland without the agreement of the majority.

The Agreement was described as 'direct rule with a heavy green tinge'. Many people praised the efforts, in a roundabout way, of the New Ireland Forum in bringing about the Agreement. Dr Conor Cruise O'Brien said:

> What distresses me is that what has been obtained by Garret FitzGerald is that at which Mr. Haughey is aiming: a deal

between Dublin and London achieved over the heads of the majority in Northern Ireland against their known wishes, and to be imposed on them against their will. That is the deal that Mr. Haughey is aiming at, and that is the deal that Garret has got. I thought it was a rotten deal, while Mr. Haughey was trying for it, and I still think it's a rotten deal, even though it is Garret who has got it. It is rotten, and extremely dangerous, because it sets up rules for governing a population which are known to be repudiated by the representatives of the population.

Mary Robinson acknowledged that the Unionists had it coming because of their intransigence:

As the majority population, who have down the years wielded power within Northern Ireland, they have been very ungenerous; they have been very unimaginative; they have not been prepared to create the conditions for promoting peace and stability. They are, to a very real extent, the authors of their own misfortunes.

However, Mary Robinson recognised that creativity and ingenuity was what was needed to move the situation on. Some green-hat thinking in order to end the strife:

That having been said, we now have to create a method of living together on this island. It is fair to say that the Unionists in particular, and the majority community as a whole, have received an enormous cultural shock from this Anglo-Irish Agreement. It is fair to say, as so many of them have said, that it was worse than their worst fears and that they were very fearful about it in advance. I believe that they are now potentially open to hard, tough talking.

The blue hat calls for reason. It is the summing-up-at-the-end hat. The Anglo-Irish Agreement came close to collapse on many occasions, not least with Margaret Thatcher's 'Out, out, out' speech when she first saw the ideas proposed by the New Ireland Forum:

> I have made it quite clear—and so did Mr. Prior when he was Secretary of State for Northern Ireland—that a unified Ireland was one solution that is out. A second solution was confederation of two states. That is out. A third solution was joint authority. That is out. That is a derogation from sovereignty. We made that quite clear when the Report was published.

Irish unity – that is out! Are you out of your mind? A two-state federation – that is outlandish! Not by a long chalk. Joint authority – that is out! Downright outrageous.

> A derogation of sovereignty.
> The slippery slope.
> A foot in the door.
> The thin edge of the wedge.
> Once the camel pokes its nose into the tent
> the next thing it has moved in.
> Give them an inch, and they'll take a mile.

She did shift her viewpoint, owing to the persistence of Garret FitzGerald, and finally agreed to sign on the dotted line at a later stage.

I am not sure it is easy to summarise the ideology of the two sides as they held such different perspectives. Garret FitzGerald was keen for Margaret Thatcher to see what the Irish dimension could bring to bear on the ending of the Troubles while Margaret Thatcher was determined to find a military solution and was not at all keen to embrace the Anglo-Irish dimension. Ultimately the Anglo-Irish Agreement failed to unify the province, but, as John Hume commented, it created a framework for the Good Friday Agreement and paved the way to peace. Peter Hadden summed up the Anglo-Irish Agreement as an 'obstacle' on the way:

> The Protestant reaction did not force Thatcher to scrap the Agreement. But it rendered it stillborn. The two governments could maintain it on paper but they were left in no doubt that a settlement would have to come via some other route and that the Anglo Irish Agreement was more of an obstacle than a staging post on the way.

De Bono's Thinking Hats would not be sufficiently robust to help the negotiators come up with a winning formula that would help to heal an intractable ethnopolitical conflict. The unique advantage in using this tool is that everyone in the group is able to look at the problem through the same lens rather that donning the red hat and becoming irate and emotional. The problem with the two main Northern Irish parties was that each side was locked into a two-hat colour mentality: orange and green. This meant that a wider perspective could not be gained and instead opinion became polarised.

So in Northern Ireland De Bono's hats were the Orangemen's bowler hats worn when they are marching. This is some research I found on the internet about the bowler:

> The bowler is a hard felt hat with a rounded crown which was originally created in 1849 for the British soldier and politician Edward Coke. Later it would come to be worn as work dress by the officers of the Queen's Guards. Originally called the iron hat, the bowler was heavier than other hats, serving as an early version of the hard hat. In Victorian

times, the bowler was a lower middle/working class hat and was typically worn by valets and butlers.

De Bono's hats were the IRA's black berets. I found this information online:

> The black beret has its origins with the French 70th Chasseurs Alpins who influenced the British Royal Tank Corps going back to 1918. General Sir Hugh Jamieson Elles, together with Colonel Fuller came up with the idea of a black beret for the Royal Tank Corps. Black was selected as the colour because it was least likely to show oil stains, something which tank crewmen of that time (and now) could appreciate.

De Bono's hats were the RUC's (former police force of Northern Ireland) helmets with their crown, harp and shamrock emblem. After the rebranding of the Royal Ulster Constabulary a new emblem was agreed upon; it featured Saint Patrick's Saltire surrounded by a harp, a crown, a shamrock, an olive branch, the scales of justice and a torch. It symbolised both the shared and different traditions of the two communities.

De Bono's hats were the maroon berets of the Parachute Regiment.

Each player in the Troubles had his own particular hat and was defined by what it represented. Nobody wanted to try on anyone else's hat for size, and therefore a stalemate was created.

Thursday, 17 September 1998

Dear Diary,
The nursery teachers were all in a little huddle this morning. Catriona, my nursery assistant, was moonlighting as an amateur child psychologist and was spouting something about a new resource she had got hold of – an adaptation of Trivial Pursuit designed to teach social skills. I suppose that's something to look forward to whenever my programme permits it.

Pierre Bourdieu was a French sociologist and philosopher. He theorised the dynamics of power in society and how the social order is transferred and perpetuated down through the generations:

> To change the world, one has to change the ways of worldmaking, that is, the vision of the world, and the practical operations by which groups are produced and reproduced.

The War of The Ghosts or Ghosts of Christmases Past
Plant memories or false memories in a person's mind.
    Sir Frederic Bartlett, a British psychologist, used the following story as the basis of one of his famous memory experiments. The students who were unfamiliar with North American tales tended to reconstruct the story in a way that resonated with their core belief schemas, and there he proved that the stories we tell are often reconstructed in order to accommodate our world view.
    One night two young men from Egulac went down to the river to hunt seals, and while they were there it became foggy and calm. Then they heard war-cries and they thought: 'Maybe this is a warparty.' They escaped to the shore and hid behind a log. Now canoes came up and they heard the noise of paddles and saw one canoe coming up to them. There were five men in the canoe and they said:

'What do you think? We wish to take you along. We are going up the river to make war on the people.'
One of the young men said, 'I have no arrows.'
'Arrows are in the canoe,' they said.
'I will not go along. I might be killed. My relatives do not know where I have gone. But you,' he said, turning to the other, 'may go with them.'
So one of the young men went, but the other returned home.
And the warriors went on up the river to a town on the other side of Kalama. The people came down to the water and they began to fight, and many were killed. But presently the young man heard one of the warriors say, 'Quick, let us go home; that Indian has been hit.' Now he thought: 'Oh, they are ghosts.' He did not feel sick, but they said he had been shot.
So the canoes went back to Egulac and the young man went ashore to his house and made a fire. And he told everybody and said: 'Behold I accompanied the ghosts, and we went to fight. Many of our fellows were killed, and many of those who attacked us were killed. They said I was hit, and I did not feel sick.'
He told it all, and then he became quiet. When the sun rose he fell down. Something black came out of his mouth. His face became contorted. The people jumped up and cried.
He was dead.

English literature students who have studied *Macbeth* will have learned about the supernatural world of the weird witches on the blasted heath who conjured up spells and chanted, 'Double, double, toil and trouble; | Fire burn, and cauldron bubble,' and would probably have no problem in recalling a detail about ghosts, but most people would invariably filter out this notion. Bartlett was not surprised when he read the retellings of the story and found that some of the students wrote that the 'boy foamed at the mouth, that it was a spirit coming out of the boy. Sometimes reference was made to paddling although the word paddling was not used in the original script. Bartlett also referred to the 'curious preservation of the trivial'.

Chinese whispers is where a statement: 'Send reinforcements, the enemy is advancing on the right flank', becomes: 'Send three and fourpence, we're going to a dance'.

Our schemas are formed from our assumptions of the world, and when something challenges our basic assumptions we find it hard to accept.

Those scribes who wrote the Anglo-Irish Agreement were not tuned in to the fact that the Unionist people view Ulster as their province, a distinct entity from the Republic. The date 1690 is of crucial importance to them because that is the year that Prince William of Orange defeated King James II at the Battle of the Boyne. They remain stuck in the drama of that battle and seek to preserve its memory as some kind of sacred victory of Protestantism over Catholicism. Each year the Battle of the Boyne is celebrated and there is no more important date in the Protestant calendar. In fact, the first two weeks of July is called the builders' fortnight because many firms take this period as their annual holiday.

The twelfth of July is a public holiday and is known as Orangemen's Day, Orange Day, the Glorious Twelfth or just the Twelfth, although the battle was actually fought on the 1st July. Like the students who reconstructed *The War of The Ghosts* in their own terms, the Orangemen used this victory as the main building block of their identity. It is said that human beings are like the iron filings on a piece of paper with a magnet beneath it: the magnet entices the filings to follow it. In the same way, our culture has a powerful influence upon us, and we may not realise that we are being pulled in a particular direction. In fact as the army chaplain George Story (1691) commented, the Williamite forces were by no means a well trained army but a mixture of English and Dutch raw recruits and Ulster men whom he described as:

> 'Half-naked with sabre and pistols hanging from their belts, like a horde of Tartars.'

At the time of the battle Britain was still using the Julian calendar, and in 1752 when Britain introduced the Gregorian calendar the dates were recalculated and the first became the twelfth. Murals in Protestant areas often depict William mounted on a white horse, brandishing a sword in his right arm and galloping across the river like Macbeth and Banquo in Shakespeare's play who, when routing the rebel, showed remarkable bravery:

> As cannons overcharged with double cracks,
> So they doubly redoubled strokes upon the foe

In fact, William of Orange had sustained a wound from a bullet fired from a Jacobite cannon and his right arm was in a sling. It is also reported that his horse was stuck in the mud and needed to be rescued, and said horse was probably not white but chestnut in colour.

1690 had a wider agenda. The head of the Catholic Church, Pope Alexander VIII, supported William because he was opposed to Louis XIV's supremacy in Europe and wanted to side with France's enemies. When William landed at Carrickfergus an onlooker marvelled at his ample arsenal:

> There being no less than seven hundred sail of ships in it, mostly laden with provisions and ammunition. The great numbers of coaches, waggons, baggage horses and the like

is almost incredible to be supplied from England, or any of the biggest nations in Europe. I cannot think that any army of Christendom hath the like.

Macbeth called the witches 'imperfect speakers', and perhaps we are imperfect historians. Sometimes the so-called facts of the past are indeed more like fabrications.

Friday, 18 September 1998

Dear Diary,
Today I realised that although I can read thousands of books, my understanding of them will be limited, so that depressed me. I won't be able to understand metaphors, and, honestly, I am disappointed at this. So phrases like 'walking on air', 'they bounced around some idea', 'keeping her head above water', 'the fly in the ointment', 'a fly on the wall' and 'walking on air' will be wasted on me.

One of the nursery assistants used a strange expression this morning when she was speaking to my mother, 'they are all tarred with the same brush'. I find it ironic (yes, I have my moments to employ figurative speech) that Schopler uses an iceberg metaphor to explain autism. The problem as I see it is that too many academic pedants are writing books about autism and not letting autistic children speak for themselves. Then teachers and teaching assistants apply this model as if they are all the same and with the same level of disability. According to the dictionary an iceberg is: 'A large floating mass of ice detached from a glacier or ice sheet and carried out to sea'. These example sentences were given:

'The environment in the Antarctic is magnificent with glaciers, icebergs and ice floes on a scale which is awe-inspiring.

'Sea ice is frozen salt water, and when natural forces break it into pieces, the larger ones are called not icebergs but ice floes.'

There is also an expression used called 'the tip of the iceberg' which is defined as 'the small perceptible part of a much larger situation or problem that remains hidden'. In Schopler's theory the specific behaviour is itemised as: seems lazy, unmotivated, waits for prompts and is overdependent. In the part of the iceberg that is not visible the possible reasons for this behaviour are given as: an unawareness of other people, a poor concept of time, being unmotivated by usual rewards and not understanding future rewards. I, for one, do not believe that my behaviour can be mapped onto an iceberg metaphor. In some ways the word 'iceberg' suggests coldness and detachment, which I am uncomfortable with. And, in turn, our caregivers are tasked with turning into detectives, always trying to find out our triggers and guiding us away from potential pitfalls. Is it that they want us to be like them and accept their idea of socialisation, not shouting out loud, not getting frustrating, not bumping into anyone else's words? Do they not understand that we are not on the same linguistic highway ... We are on a detour, and sometimes on a detour you see the most curious things.

Bend it Like Blair
In 2006 Unionists and Nationalists were deadlocked over talks to restore the devolved institutions. Tony Blair says that to avoid a complete collapse of the process he sometimes lied to the parties. He said that he took 'horrendous' chances with what he told the respective parties and that he stretched the truth on occasions 'past breaking point'.

Tony Blair admitted to 'bending and distorting' the truth as prime minister but said that a degree of manipulation and distortion were necessary to govern and that voters accepted that. 'Politicians are obliged from time to time to conceal the full truth, to bend it and even distort it, where the interests of the bigger strategic goal demand it be done. Without operating with some subtlety at this level, the job would be well-nigh impossible.'

Discussing his approach to the truth he suggested that, at a deeper level, voters retained trust in him because he was trying to do his best for them.

He said that the public discriminate between politicians they do not trust at a shallow level – 'ie, pretty much all of them' – and those that they do not trust at a more profound level.

Different Number Plates Same Car
Each Agreement was just the same car with different number plates, and the people who mattered, the people from the two main communities, didn't want to test drive it never mind buy it – even if it was a souped-up DeLorean; what worked for other agreement processes did not work for Northern Ireland.

Other Models
The Dayton Accords brokered peace in Bosnia and Herzegovina, and the talks were chaired by Richard Holbrooke. Holbrooke said he would not go to Geneva because he considered it the city of failed diplomacies. Instead the talks took place at Wright-Patterson Air Force Base, Dayton, Ohio. Dayton is sometimes referred to as the diadem of Ohio, the cradle of aviation and the aviation capital of the world. It was there that the Wright brothers, Orville and Wilbur, developed their flying machine into a fixed-wing aircraft. It is the city that invented night aerial photography, free-fall parachutes, crop dusting, pressurised cabins and landing lights.

Bosnians, Croats and Serbs had to be accommodated by Holbrooke. He said he wanted to be away from the press but accessible, and it was a site that worked. The public formed a ring around the base, prayed for a peaceful outcome and placed candles of peace in windows. Instead of endless squabbling over details Holbrooke took the reins, he took the initiative; he energised the process. He called it an imperfect peace. There were mistakes. Three armies, three presidents, two police forces and a weak central government. There is, however, a difference between agreement and implementation: all the presidents said they wanted peace, but what about the war criminals? 'There's nothing in the agreement that obligates the parties to go out and find them, but there are certain obligations to deal with them under certain circumstances. It's technical ...'

It was initialled by the Republic of Bosnia and Herzegovina, the Republic of Croatia and the Federal Republic of Yugoslavia (FRY). The Accord was witnessed by representatives of the Contact Group nations – the United States, Britain, France, Germany and Russia – and the European Union Special Negotiator.

The very skill of the draftsmen made the first article of the Belfast Agreement so ambiguous that it was no surprise that there were aspersions of doublespeak cast over the entire accord.

The same impasses, the same cul-de-sacs, false dawns, setbacks, the same dead ends and blank walls, so many late-night meetings, last-minute phone calls, so many back channels. The same old hindrances, obstacles, misunderstandings and everyone looking askance – I ask you. The same issues, the same old chestnuts, the worn-out arguments. There was no moving forward, no negotiation, no consensus, no laissez-passer, just cross words, crossed wires and stumbling blocks until everyone had fallen out; no one wanting to give an inch, not even a centimetre or a millimetre.

No one could draw a line in the sand. A small room can only contain so much hatred and leaves little wriggle room. One side wanted the border and the union while the other side wanted to break the link with Britain and get rid of the border. What do you do with two irreconcilable notions? Two hostile groups whose incremental steps to peace could be halted by an accusation that one side was being given preferential treatment over the other? And one key figure had a crow to pick with another key figure, and no one was going to forget the past or let it go away or get off lightly, God forbid. There were no get-out-of-jail-free cards, no talk of burying the hatchet or smoking the peace pipe. No, there were too many smoking guns, too many unsolved crimes, too much collusion and too many cover-ups. No one could see eye to eye when their hearts said we want an eye for an eye, a life for a life and somebody must pay for the loss of my loved ones. Most of all everyone wanted the truth, the unvarnished truth, the warts-and-all truth, the undistorted truth. The way the two communities lived cheek by jowl made it impossible to partition them. It would be like trying to draw borders around the black and white squares of a chessboard. Why are people so unobliging – living so close to each other and making it impossible for the map-makers to split them? In a game of chess the pieces know their place and can only move in their predetermined styles; the bishop can move diagonally, the king can only move one square in any direction, the rook can move any number of squares along any rank or file, the queen can move any number of squares in any direction, pawns can only move straight ahead and the knight can jump other pieces and move horizontally two places and vertically one place or vice versa. Unlike a game of chess, in the NI peace process, the only game is stalemate.

No one was being open and transparent; it was all smoke and mirrors and sleight of hand and legerdemain. No stone should be left unturned, but could we handle the truth? If we got the truth, would it destroy us?

Monday, 21 September 1998

Dear Diary,
There was some kind of discussion going on about autistic children having a presumed relationship with Thomas the Tank Engine, a fictional steam locomotive. The little blue engine has a cheeky face on the front and his expressions are easy to understand. Miss Watts was reading out that autistic children love the bright colours of the engines in the books and videos, and that each story or video is easy to understand. This is some dialogue from one of the videos where the engines discuss how to stop Diesel 10:

> Toby: What's important is to stand up on our own wheels to Diesel.
> Henry: Toby's right. Diesel knows that the lost engine in the legend really exists.
> James: *What* engine?
> Percy: *What* legend?
> Henry: Of an engine whose magic makes her more powerful than Diesel will ever be, that's why he wants to find her.
> Percy: Then we'd better find her first.
> James: [*comes out of the shed*] Leave it to the big engines, Percy.
> Thomas: Little Engines can do big things, especially when they have nice blue paint like me.

I ask you – an engine with a smiley face! I shudder at the thought of these amateur psychologists holding out rows of emoticons ranging from happy to sad. I can hear one of them putting John, the other autistic child, through his paces:

'How are you today, little icebergie? Why are you lazy? Why are you unmotivated? Why are you waiting for prompts? Why are you overdependent?'

Then she will implement one of her programmes to tackle the behaviour; she will drag him through some autistic intervention in order to motivate him as the hidden part, the part below the surface which you do not see, has a poor concept of time and is not motivated by the usual rewards. Under special educational needs policy in the Education Order 1996 my special needs must be addressed. These teachers seem to know their rights, but I have my rights too:

> In all cases the school should remember that the rights of the child are paramount. (Children (Northern Ireland) Order 1995)

In new Good-Friday-Agreement speak everyone is always spouting off about his or her rights as enshrined at its centre. They've even established two institutions: the Equality Commission and the Human Rights Commission to guarantee that the new government is 'founded on principles of full respect for, and equality of, civil, political, social and cultural rights'.

But I wonder if their autistic programmes and pathways of care will be paramount? I agree with Eric Erikson's views on childhood regimentation: he referred to introducing 'the never-silent metronome of routine into the impressionable baby'. Like an Indian guru he could see through the conditioning that prevailed in schools. Erikson also said that 'political systems have thrived on the provocation of manifold and morbid doubt'. I will never become the so-called successful man in the material world, but these programmes will help me to become a well-adjusted autistic person. Every day I will line up my overturned figures and play another game of soldiers.

> 'I care not for the siren voices of those who will raise them against me.'
>
> Ian Paisley

In Book XII of Homer's *Odyssey*, Circe warns Odysseus about the sirens, two mythical sisters, from the south coast of Italy whose singing entices sailors to the degree that they crash their ships and drown. Odysseus ordered his men to stuff their ears with wax to drown out their songs, and he got them to tie him to the mast so he wouldn't be carried away by the alluring women-birds. When Ian Paisley delivered a speech at the Democratic Unionist Party's Annual Conference in 1994 he declared that, 'A true patriot and statesman must also be a watchman.' He referred to himself as a modern Ezekiel who relayed God's prophecies to the people. Ezekiel, a sixth century BC prophet, saw himself as a watchman who was sent by God to warn the people of forthcoming disasters which their pig-headedness and idolatry had brought about:

> Son of man, speak to the children of thy people, and say unto them, When I bring the sword upon a land, if the people of the land take a man of their coasts, and set him for their watchman: If when he seeth the sword come upon the land, he blow the trumpet, and warn the people; Then whosoever heareth the sound of the trumpet, and taketh not warning; if the sword come, and take him away, his blood shall be upon his own head. He heard the sound of the trumpet, and took not warning; his blood shall be upon him. But he that taketh warning shall deliver his soul. But if the watchman see the sword come, and blow not the trumpet, and the people be not warned; if the sword come, and take any person from among them, he is taken away in his iniquity; but his blood will I require at the watchman's hand. It is as a faithful watchman that I want to address you today. I care not about popularity. I care not for the siren voices of those who will raise them against me. I care not for the strength of the opposition I only care that the blood of

the people I represent will not be upon my garments in the day of final judgment before my God.

James Joyce's *Ulysses* Episode 11 is entitled Sirens.

BRONZE BY GOLD HEARD THE HOOFIRONS, STEELY-RINGING IMPERthnthn thnthnthn.
Chips, picking chips off rocky thumbnail, chips.
Horrid! And gold flushed more.
A husky fifenote blew.
Blew. Blue bloom is on the
Gold pinnacled hair.
A jumping rose on satiny breasts of satin, rose of Castile.
Trilling, trilling : Idolores.
Peep! Who's in the ... peepofgold?
Tink cried to bronze in pity.
And a call, pure, long and throbbing. Longindying call.
Decoy. Soft word. But look! The bright stars fade. O rose!
Notes irruping answer. Castille. The morn is breaking.
Jingle jingle jaunted jingling.
Coin rang. Clock clacked.
Avowal. *Sonnez*. I could. Rebound of garter. Not leave thee.
Smack. *La che!* Thigh smack. Avowal. Warm. Sweetheart, goodbye!
Jingle. Bloo.

Never, Never, Never.
Never is an adverb of frequency, and repetition of the same word three times is a form of rhetorical speech. In *Introducing NLP: Psychological Skills for Understanding and Influencing People*, O'Connor and Seymour explain modal operators of possibility.

These are rules of conduct beyond which we believe we cannot or must not go. These modal operators, they argue, 'set limits governed by unspoken rules'. Instead of framing your statements in modal operators they suggest we should ask, 'What stops me from doing this thing that I have convinced myself that I cannot do?' Fritz Perls, the man who invented Gestalt therapy, said that when someone says they cannot do a thing it means they just won't do it. He had good results using this rather abrupt reframing methodology.

Mike Bundrant, a retired psychotherapist, itemised four words that can kill a relationship: never, always, can't and should. In discussing 'never' he wrote:

> Unless you're psychic and know the entire future, saying that something will never happen or someone will never accomplish something makes you seem like a know-it-all. And, when what you said would never happen comes true, you come off as untrustworthy.

Instead of 'You'll never' he suggests 'It's hard to imagine that you'll', and instead of 'I'll never' you could say 'I don't think I could bring myself to' and 'That never happens' could become, 'I haven't ever noticed.'

But in 1985 Ian Paisley was more of an inciter than a psychic, and he hadn't the benefit of neurolinguistic programming or maps and filters or present states and desired states or pacing and leading. He had no eye or other accessing cues, no submodalities, no chaining anchors or collapsing anchors, no snakes and ladders, no stepping up and stepping down, no metaprogrammes, just 'No surrender'. He was going to have his cake and eat it. This Anglo-Irish thing took the biscuit and he would crush it. He smelt a rat. Margaret Thatcher was in cahoots with the Taoiseach. Margaret Thatcher was hand-in-glove with Garrett FitzGerald all along; she was the iron hand in the velvet glove. She led him by the nose and he led her by the hand, and now they were holding hands and selling out Ulster. Their little tête-à-têtes out of earshot, their little heart-to-heart discussions in Chequers drinking tea and eating crumpets, and all the while she was pretending to be just exploring options. She said she wouldn't impose an Agreement; she said she couldn't pull proposals out of the hat like a magician at a children's party. She said she couldn't impose solutions, that there had to be agreement, but all the while the devious strumpet was betraying the Protestant people. There was no shortage of proposals – the way to hell is paved with good proposals. There was no shortage of Secretaries of State who had a plethora of proposals; a pile of propositions had been put forward by William Whitelaw, Francis Pym, Merlyn Rees, Roy Mason, Humphrey Atkins, followed by Jim Prior, Douglas Hurd, Tom King and Peter Brooke.

My Mother's Diary
Monday, 14 September 1998

Dear Diary,
This was the worst day of my life. I am feeling so low. I know Patrick is a quiet, sensitive child, but I had no idea that he is autistic. I am in the first stage of the Kübler-Ross Grief Cycle: denial, and I will stay in this stage for a long time. When I carried him out this morning he was a normal baby, and now he has a disability – a label, a disabling label. After becoming an expert on Winnicott and Klein I am now having to learn and implement a new way of coping. When I woke up this morning I was a mother, now I'm a carer. Instead of looking forward to my son taking his place in the world of medicine, law or teaching, all I have to look forward to are endless meetings, endless therapies, motor and sensory interventions, 'social stories' and 'comic strip conversations', special schools, autism friendly cinemas, and so forth.

If the Anglo-Irish Agreement was written as a Kennings poem it would sound like this:

Status of Northern Ireland

Article 1
Affirmer only majority can change status
Recogniser that there is no wish to change
Declarer that united Ireland if majority wish

Article 2
Deliberator on political matters
Deliberator on security and related matters
Deliberator on legal matters
Deliberator on cross-border cooperation
No lessening of sovereignty

Article 3
Meeting at ministerial or official level

Article 4
Maker of the rights and identities of the two traditions
Maker of peace, stability and prosperity throughout the island of Ireland
Promoter of reconciliation
Respecter of human rights
Cooperator against terrorism
Developer of economy, society and culture

Article 5
Accommodator of the rights and identities of the two traditions

Protector of human rights
Preventer of discrimination
Fosterer of cultural heritage

Article 6
Organiser of the Standing Advisory Commission on Human Rights
Organiser of the Fair Employment Agency
Organiser of the Equal Opportunities Commission
Organiser of the Policy Authority for Northern Ireland
Organiser of the Police Complaints Board

Article 7
Supporter of security policy
Supporter of relations between the security forces and the community
Supporter of prisons policy

Article 8
Dealer of issues concerning criminal law
Harmoniser of criminal law in North and South
Restorer of confidence in administration of justice

Article 9
Enhancer of cross-border cooperation between Royal Ulster Constabulary and Garda Siochána

Article 10
Promoter of economic and social development in areas which have suffered the most

Article 11
Planner for future review
Inter-parliamentary relations

Article 12
Foreshadower of Anglo-Irish parliamentary body

Article 13
Not legal until signed

Bernadette McAliskey commented that Sinn Féin was 'hanging on by its fingernails'. She used the analogy of a funnel to describe Gerry Adams' diminishing choices. She argued that the clever British had him over a barrel; like a fly in the funnel of a wine bottle, the closer he got to the lip the narrower the funnel got and the 'nice smell wafting from the bottle' made it impossible to climb out.

Some people who objected to the Anglo-Irish Agreement said that it was old wine in new skins. In Matthew, Jesus responds to criticism being levelled against his disciples for not fasting by pointing out that there will be a time for fasting in the future, after his death. He uses two interesting metaphors which express the need to move on from the past:

> No one puts a piece of unshrunk cloth on an old garment; for the patch tears away from the garment, and a worse tear is made.
> Neither is new wine put into old wineskins. If it is, the skins burst and the wine is spilled and the skins are destroyed. But new wine is put into fresh wineskins, and so both are preserved.

The wine of the Anglo-Irish Agreement tasted bitter to the Unionists; it turned to vinegar. Margaret Thatcher had betrayed them.

My Mother's Diary
Tuesday, 15 September 1998

Dear Diary,
After I wallow in denial for a long while, and if I play my cards right, I will move to anger, the second stage. I would just like to point out that you don't move along the stages in a formulaic way and sometimes the predominating emotion is tainted with another one and in my case it was blame. , I want someone to blame – starting with my mother, my absent father, genetics, epigenetics, prenatal environment, perinatal environment, lack of vitamin D, lead, mercury vaccines; I have a myriad of people and things to be angry at. I am even angry that the staff were collecting money for one of the babies who has been diagnosed with leukaemia. Would they be collecting money for my autistic baby?

I associate patchwork with a rustic setting where poverty is a virtue and wealth is a vice. The word 'patchwork' is a needlework term which means to sew together pieces of cloth of various shapes, textures and colours in order to make a quilt. That is the mass noun meaning, but you can also use it as a modifier and talk about a patchwork quilt. I just picked up an events guide for the Roe Valley Arts & Cultural Centre which contained the following advertisement for a workshop:

Beginner's Patchwork Workshops with Gortnaghey Community Association led by experienced patchwork quilt tutor Sandra Montgomery.

On the flyer there is a picture of a quilt and I can see green, yellow and pink flowers.

> Quilting is not for the faint-hearted.
> No! It's painstaking piecing it all together.
> A square here, square there, an eye there.
> A tooth there, a bombing here, a maiming there!

> People opened their hearts to make this quilt.
> Civil rights marchers marched to make this quilt.
> British Army Sergeant Michael Willetts was killed by the IRA to make this quilt.
> Innocent men were rounded up at dawn to make this quilt.
> They were banged into prison to make this quilt.
> Bin lids were banged on pavements to make this quilt.
> Pavements were torn up and thrown at British soldiers to make this quilt.
> The Anglo-Irish Agreement was torn up to make this quilt.
> Rubber bullets blinded children to make this quilt.
> Fathers and sons were shot dead to make this quilt.
> Internment was used to make this quilt.
> Diplock courts were used to make this quilt.
> Hunger strikes took place to make this quilt.

Paul Arthur remarked that 'After 1972, Northern Ireland became what one commentator called "a kind of adventure playground for constitutional initiatives".' The word playground means 'an area of land where children can play, especially at a school or in a park'. It is well known that playgrounds can be an area where children play but where they also engage in sham fights, fisticuffs and shadow-boxing. A playground is a place for scraps and name calling, settling scores and establishing the pecking order. The run-ins and set-tos are the dry runs for the assembly room, the auction room, the back room, the boardroom, the classroom, the darkroom, the locker room, the mailroom, the newsroom, the operating room, the poolroom, the restroom, the stockroom, the stateroom, the staffroom, the sunroom, the waiting room, the weights room and the workroom. These puerile pugilists could be tomorrow's prizefighters or hoodlums, tomorrow's lawmakers or lawbreakers, tomorrow's law enforcers or housebreakers, tomorrow's doctors or drug pushers, tomorrow's entrepreneurs or dropouts, tomorrow's computer programmers or con artists, tomorrow's presidents or plagiarists. Who knows?

In the preface to *Gods and Fighting Men* by Lady Gregory, W. B. Yeats wrote that 'Children play at being great and wonderful people, at the ambitions they will put away for one reason or another before they grow into ordinary men and women.' He goes on to say that humans could do the greatest deeds if they were not afraid of falling foul of the law or disobeying the laws of nature. He describes the Fianna, or fighting men, as men who accessed their power and are 'set in a world so fluctuating and dream-like, that nothing can hold them from being all that the heart desires.' He writes that:

> The men of Dea fought against the mis-shapen Fomor, as Finn fights against the Cat-Heads and the Dog-Heads; and when they are overcome at last by men, they make themselves houses in the hearts of hills that are like the houses of men.

The greatest of the Red Branch Knights was Cuchulain, and Cathbad prophesied that, 'The boy who takes up the spear and shield of manhood on this day will become the greatest and most renowned of all the warriors of Ireland, men will follow at his call to the world's end, and his enemies will shudder at the thunder of his chariot wheels, and the harpers shall sing of him while green Ireland yet rises above the sea …' Cuchulain begged King Conor Mac Nessa to bestow on him the 'arms of manhood that day'.

An adventure playground is: 'a playground containing objects or structures such as ropes, slides, and tunnels, for children to play on or in'. The playground metaphor sounds strange at first, and some may find that to refer to Ulster as a playground for constitutional conjecture is somewhat discordant. After 3,500 deaths, maiming and mayhem, both civilian and military, from 1969 onwards it suggests a battleground rather than a playground. So 'Nero fiddled while Rome burned', and as the politicians trundled out framework after framework, initiative after initiative, Ulster suffered and lives were shortened.

And before Ireland was an adventure playground for constitutional proposals it was an adventure playground for wars. Some of the stories are mythical, but it can be said that from the beginning of time Ireland was defined by her wars. The history of Ireland is a history punctuated by battles, invasions, internecine conflicts, family feuds and rebellions.

According to Mary Frances Cusack there were five invasions as recorded in the *Leabhar Gabhála*; the earliest invasion was before the biblical flood. According to the *Leabhar Gabhála*, the first colonist was a Greek woman called Cessair who arrived with forty-nine other women and three men. So from the very beginning things were out of balance – too many women and too few men! Cessair sailed to Ireland, but before she did that she consulted an oracle and he told her to take with her three men: Fintan mac Bóchra, Bith and Ladra. It was a rough journey but Cessair was protected by a favourable wind because she had made an offering of two bulls to Poseidon before she left Athens. Unfortunately the men died quite young; they were used to olive groves and Mediterranean weather and they weren't able to cope in bogs and marshes. They couldn't catch a hare or skin a boar or give chase with a hound. They were a maritime people and they had no experience of tilling the land. Cessair felt no connection with the Greek Gods, no protection from Poseidon, and there wasn't enough time to connect with the local deities who were mostly rough bog deities. The Greek colony didn't thrive and Cessair died shortly after Fintan. She was buried in Connacht and a cairn was raised in her honour, while Fintan is said to have morphed into a salmon and then an eagle.

Next to come ashore to the Green Isle was Partholan, his sons, daughter and a thousand followers. It is said that they cleared the plains and cut down the forests. According to folklore this tribe was wiped out by the plague in the course of a week. Tallaght is a town on the Southside of Dublin, and the name comes from the Irish *támh leacht* meaning plague pit.

After the Partholians came the Neimhidhians led by Nemedh. This tribe had to do battle with the Formorians, a pugilistic and troublesome tribe who also practised piracy. The Firbolgs were the fourth tribe to colonise Ireland, and it is said that they divided the island into five provinces. The Tuatha de Danann was the fifth band of colonisers, and according to mythology they were a royal dynasty who possessed supernatural powers. It is even alleged that the people believed they were Gods and worshipped them. They had four items which assured their pre-eminence: *Lia Fáil*, the stone of destiny; the cauldron of the Daghda; the sword of Nuada; and the spear of Lugh. They defeated the Formorians at the battle of Moytura.

At the first battle of Moytura a fierce Firbolg, Streng, cut off Nuada's arm. The two sides negotiated a truce. Dian Cecht forged a silver hand and Nuada became known as Nuada of the Silver Hand.

Because he had a physical blemish he was unable to continue as king, so Bres, a handsome Formorian king, was elected instead. Bres was a bad king and he enslaved the Tuatha de Danann. There were some more showdowns and face-offs which involved a one-eyed giant called Balor killing Bres and restoring harmony. As is the case nowadays, so it was the case then; Irish tribal wars were and still are settled by the sword rather than with dialogue. Even the mythological ancestors were handier with a sword than a plough, quicker to brandish a spear than forge a truce. All parleys were preambles to skulduggery; they were better at knavery that being neighbourly. Cessair would have turned in her cairn if she had had an inkling of these wars and internecine squabbles. Above all else the Greeks valued their gods who snatched victory from the jaws of defeat and brought forth order from chaos. Olympus was the home of the Twelve Olympian gods who defeated the Titans. Zeus was the leader of the gods and they met in a pantheon. The other gods were Hera, Hestia, Demeter, Poseidon, Athena, Apollo, Artemis, Hermes, Aphrodite, Ares and Hephaestus. In Pieria the nine Muses live: Calliope (epic poetry), Clio (history), Erato (love poetry), Euterpe (music), Melpomene (tragedy), Polyhymnia (hymns), Terpsichore (dance), Thalia (comedy) and Urania (astronomy).

Pre-Christian Ulster would be unrecognisable today. It was covered with forests of trees and contained many bogs and lakes. A great dyke which consisted of a series of defensive networks was built to demarcate Ulster as a separate province. It is known as the Black Pig's Dyke or *Claí na Muice Duibhe* and runs all the way from Bundoran in County Donegal to South Armagh.

The Milesians were the Gaels who migrated from Iberia and colonised Ireland. The name *Míl Espáine* is an Irish version of *Miles Hispaniae* or Soldier of Hispania. It is said that the Gaels can trace their lineage back to Adam, and that Fénius Farsaid, a descendant of Noah, lived in Scythia. He, along with another seventy-one chieftains, built the Tower of Babel. Fénius' son, Ned, married Scota and their son was called Góidel Glas. Góidel's offspring are said to have wandered the earth for hundreds of years until they reached Iberia. In Iberia Breogán, a descendant of Góidel, founded the city of Brigantia and built a tower there. His son Íth spied Ireland from the top of the tower and decided to sail there and see the island for himself. Three of the Tuatha de Danann kings, Mac Cecht, Mac Cuill and Mac Gréine met and dialogued with him. However, he was murdered and his men returned to Iberia. But this was not the end of the Gaels in Ireland: Íth's relatives returned and marched to Tara. On the way they met Banba, Fódla and Ériu who promised them good fortune if they named the island after one of them. At Tara the Gaels laid down their terms and the Tuatha de Danann agreed but they requested a three-day truce. They asked the Gaels to sail out beyond the ninth wave after which the Tuatha de Danann used their magical powers to conjure up a storm preventing the enemy ships return. But the Gael's resourceful bard, Amergin, calmed the wind with a verse. After another summit meeting in Tara, the Tuatha de Danann were banished to the underworld and the island was divided between Éremon and Éber Finn. It seems that to stay alive you have to stay alert, and it appears the Gaels had the upper hand.

The arrival of the Celtic people in Ireland marked the end of the Bronze Age. They introduced iron and kingship, they divided Ireland into kingdoms and they introduced Brehon Law. They brought their Druids with them, they were more philosophers than priests, who presided over sacred rituals. They were tutors and peacemakers, philosophers and sages, inventors and scientists. Their bards were highly skilled poets and musicians, and this had a civilising influence on the people. They produced poems about their history and culture, and their work was characterised by a high degree of technical excellence and devices such as half rhyme, assonance and alliteration were employed.

Thomas Francis O'Rahilly argued that the Celts did not launch a full-scale invasion but came at different stages: between 700–500 BC the Cruithne or Priteni arrived, around 500 BC the Builg or the Érainn arrived, followed by the Laigin, the Domnainn, and the Gálioin in 300 BC and finally, in 100 BC, the Goidels or Gaels.

The Goidels were divided into the Connachta and the Eóganachta. The Connachta carved out the province of Meath after defeating the Emean king at Tara. The Eóganachta settled in Munster.

Tacitus wrote that General Agricola toyed with the idea of conquering Ireland as the ports would be strategically useful: 'I have often heard Agricola declare that a single legion, with a moderate band of auxiliaries, would be enough to finish the conquest of Ireland.' In the end the Romans decided it would not be worth the effort.

And so the history of Ireland for many years was such that one tribe arrived, survived and died only to be replaced by another. In the late eighth century the Vikings landed marauding, pillaging and looting the monasteries. Brian Boru, although killed himself, defeated the Norsemen at the battle of Clontarf, 1014. Then there were the Strongbow and Norman invasions and the twelfth century English invasions. This led to seven hundred years of penal laws, harsh repression and fierce rebellions. The 1916 Easter Rising resulted in the Irish War of Independence, and after the Anglo-Irish Treaty was signed the country was partitioned and the Irish Civil War broke out.

There was a fear among Unionists that their statelet would be throttled at birth. This fear of being strangled left a deep scar on the Protestant psyche and created a siege mentality. During the Williamite Wars the city of Derry had to defend itself against the Jacobite army. The siege lasted from April 1689 to July of the same year. There are stories of how the Apprentice Boys locked the city gates in order to prevent the Jacobite army from entering. In turn, the Jacobite army mounted a blockade and no supplies were able to get into the city, and the besieged Protestants faced potential starvation. Their motto was 'No Surrender', a no surrender that has echoed down the centuries.

A siege situation involves a protracted period of suspense causing more psychological damage than physical harm. Joy Gordon has highlighted the way siege warfare impacts on civilian life:

> Siege warfare—the military blockade of a city or country to prevent goods from going in, and to prevent people from escaping—raises terribly serious problems from an ethical perspective. The principle of discrimination in Just War doctrine, and in international law, holds that in warfare the belligerents are required to discriminate between combatants and noncombatants, and may not target civilians. Yet siege warfare has precisely the opposite effect: when you cut off a city's access to food or water, those who are least able to survive the deprivation are children and infants, the elderly, the sick. At the same time, the state is likely to prioritize security, and shift resources to the military and to the political and military leadership, worsening the situation of civilians. So in siege warfare, the principle of discrimination is effectively inverted: not only is there no special protection for the civilian population, but that is precisely the population that will bear the worst costs, and within the general civilian population, those who suffer first, and worst, are those least responsible for the state's decisions—children and infants, the elderly, the sick.

Sieges, therefore, are particularly devastating for women and children who are often left at the mercy of the conquering army. In his book on ancient siege warfare, Paul Bentley Kern points out that siege warfare has been a horrific instrument of war from ancient times. He refers to the Old Testament in 701 BCE when the Assyrian king Sennacherib laid siege to Jerusalem but failed to capture the city as one example. Another example is the Trojan War, which took place between the Greeks and the Trojans (and erupted over the abduction of Helen, wife of Menelaus of Sparta). The Greeks besieged Troy for nine years and were only successful when the former tricked the latter into taking the infamous Trojan Horse into the city. And the rest is history. Yahweh was on the side of the Jews, and Poseidon, Hera and Athena were on the side of the Greeks, while Aphrodite and Ares were on the side of the Trojans. When the Germans failed to take Leningrad after a horrendous siege Hitler said, 'The god of war has gone over to the other side.' In the siege of Derry God must have been on the side of the Protestants.

The chequered history of Ireland, its wars and feuds, echoes down the centuries and is punctuated with agreements and peace initiatives. It's like a scrapbook of scraps, an album of escapades, a saga of capers, a surplus of suggestions, a plethora of proposals, a glut of initiatives; sometimes it was grist for the mill and catnip for the press and heartache for the architects of peace. As Sir John Maffey said, 'For the outside world, Dark Rosaleen has a sex appeal whereas Britain is regarded as the maiden aunt.' James Clarence Mangan translated the poem *Róisín Dubh*:

> O my dark Rosaleen,
> Do not sigh, do not weep!
> The priests are on the ocean green,
> They march along the deep.
> There's wine from the royal Pope,
> Upon the ocean green;
> And Spanish ale shall give you hope,
> My Dark Rosaleen!
> My own Rosaleen!

Shall glad your heart, shall give you hope,
Shall give you health, and help, and hope,
My Dark Rosaleen!

Over hills, and thro' dales,
Have I roam'd for your sake;
All yesterday I sail'd with sails
On river and on lake.
The Erne, at its highest flood,
I dash'd across unseen,
For there was lightning in my blood,
My Dark Rosaleen!

My own Rosaleen!
O, there was lightning in my blood,
Red lightning lighten'd thro' my blood.
My Dark Rosaleen!

All day long, in unrest,
To and fro, do I move.
The very soul within my breast
Is wasted for you, love!
The heart in my bosom faints
To think of you, my Queen,
My life of life, my saint of saints,
My Dark Rosaleen!
My own Rosaleen!
To hear your sweet and sad complaints,
My life, my love, my saint of saints,
My Dark Rosaleen!

Woe and pain, pain and woe,
Are my lot, night and noon,
To see your bright face clouded so,

Like to the mournful moon.
But yet will I rear your throne
Again in golden sheen;

'Tis you shall reign, shall reign alone,
My Dark Rosaleen!
My own Rosaleen!
'Tis you shall have the golden throne,
'Tis you shall reign, and reign alone,
My Dark Rosaleen!

Over dews, over sands,
Will I fly, for your weal:
Your holy delicate white hands
Shall girdle me with steel.
At home, in your emerald bowers,
From morning's dawn till e'en,
You'll pray for me, my flower of flowers,
My Dark Rosaleen!
My fond Rosaleen!
You'll think of me through daylight hours,
My virgin flower, my flower of flowers,
My Dark Rosaleen!

I could scale the blue air,
I could plough the high hills,
O, I could kneel all night in prayer,
To heal your many ills!
And one beamy smile from you
Would float like light between
My toils and me, my own, my true,
My Dark Rosaleen!
My fond Rosaleen!
Would give me life and soul anew,

A second life, a soul anew,
My Dark Rosaleen!

O, the Erne shall run red,
With redundance of blood,
The earth shall rock beneath our tread,
And flames wrap hill and wood,
And gun-peal and slogan-cry
Wake many a glen serene,
Ere you shall fade, ere you shall die,
My Dark Rosaleen!
My own Rosaleen!
The Judgement Hour must first be nigh,
Ere you can fade, ere you can die,
My Dark Rosaleen!

Ireland is often represented as a mother or a beautiful woman. This image was used to fire up nationalism and patriotic pride. In Irish mythology the female, the Goddess, confers valour and pluck on the warriors. Not only that, but she is the nation.

My Mother's Diary
Wednesday, 16 September 1998

Dear Diary,
I have moved up the Kübler-Ross scale at a superhuman rate for today I am bargaining with God: if I pray and go to Mass again, God might reverse this diagnosis. After all, miracles happen every day; miracles are happening in this country right now. My baby was born on the day of the Agreement – there is no such thing as coincidence, Patrick has a destiny. I am sure of that. If the Agreement flourishes, Patrick will flourish. He was born with the hand of history on his birth chart, not Hans Asperger on his birth certificate.

In *Midnight's Children* Saleem's birth was celebrated in the newspapers, politicians acknowledged him and the Prime Minister Jawaharlal Nehru wrote:

> Dear Baby Saleem, My belated congratulations on the happy accident of your moment of birth! You are the newest bearer of that ancient face of India which is also eternally young. We shall be watching over your life with the closest attention; it will be, in a sense, the mirror of our own.

Patrick received no such endorsement from the newspapers or the politicians. The fact that he was born on the same day as the Agreement did not set off a media flurry. Yet somehow I think he will have a special destiny. He has been dealt a blow by fate, but surely he will receive some special powers from the very fact that his birth coincided with the most momentous days in Ulster's history.

After so many false dawns it was clear that there could be no more quick fixes. The famous IRA slogan, 'We only have to be lucky once' was not applicable when it came to the Agreement for it seemed as if the Agreement was doomed to fail – it had more the Anna-Karenina syndrome. The opening of Tolstoy's *Anna Karenina*, 'Happy families are all alike; every unhappy family is unhappy in its own way', is one of the most famous lines in literature. Good agreements are all alike, but unworkable agreements are unworkable in their own ways. The Agreement would only triumph if each of the negotiators had the will for it to succeed, but every time a draft was aired one side poked holes in it, saw flaws in it, claimed it was a farce, a fudge and that you could drive a horse and carriage through it, and the other side said the other side was being negative, intransigent and stubborn. Tony Blair controlled the purse strings, he had the trump card, and this time no one could play the Orange card. Meanwhile he stuck to his guns and at the same time wanted the paramilitaries to decommission. He used to listen to the Fleetwood Mac song 'Tusks', which is quite apt in these circumstances. It seems The Good Friday Agreement had to be all things to all people. The lines from the song, 'Why don't you ask him if he's going to stay? Why don't you ask him if he's going away?' may have resonated with him as it was almost impossible to reach an agreement and there was always an edge to every meeting and interchange.

Tony Blair said that these four things must be obeyed and there must be no equivocation in the parties' commitment to the Agreement:

A: first and foremost, a clear and unequivocal commitment that there is an end to violence for good, on the part of republicans and loyalists alike, and that the so-called war is finished, done with, gone; that, as the Agreement says, non-violence and exclusively peaceful and democratic means are the only means used;

B: that, again as the Agreement expressly states, the cease-fires are indeed complete and unequivocal; an end to bombings, killings and beatings, claimed or unclaimed; an end to targeting and procurement of weapons; progressive abandonment and dismantling of paramilitary structures actively directing and promoting violence;
C: full co-operation with the Independent Commission on decommissioning, to implement the provisions of the Agreement; and
D: no other organisations being deliberately used as proxies for violence.

Even the seating arrangements could be contentious as certain parties did not want to sit next to certain other parties. The Unionists would next sit to the Irish or Paisley's crowd … the British had to act as a buffer between the two, then the SDLP next to Paisley, then the Irish ministers, and then Alliance. It the end and if you are a political veteran in Northern Ireland you realise there never is an endgame, the best on could say was that the Belfast Agreement was like good in places, like the curate's egg. It was more like the riddle of the strands and the pundits commented that although there was never a meeting of minds there had been some symbolic breakthroughs and there had been a learning process. None of the warring camps were going to become Facebook friends and maybe never shake hands as there was just too much baggage to shed, too many closets in the cupboard, but at least an Agreement had been hammered out.

Peacemaking Strategies in Northern Ireland
In Paul Bew's *The Making and Remaking of the Good Friday Agreement* Lijphart says, 'It may be difficult, but it is not at all impossible to achieve and maintain stable democratic government in a plural society.'

Whataboutery! What about this and what about that? That happened in the past. Give them an inch and they'll take a mile. It doesn't stack up. Nothing stacks up. One side has a crow to pluck with the other side.

In her memoir *Bad Blood* Lorna Sage wrote:

So the playground was hell: Chinese burns, pinches, slaps and kicks, and horrible games. I can still hear the noise of a thick wet skipping rope slapping the ground. There'd be a big girl at each end and you had to leap through without tripping. Joining in was only marginally less awful than being left out. It's said (truly) that most women forget the pain of childbirth; I think that we all forget the pain of being a child at school for the first time, the sheer ineptitude, as though you'll never learn to mark out your own space. It's doubly shaming – shaming to *remember* as well, to feel so sorry for your scabby little self back then in small people's purgatory.

War! war! no peace! peace is to me a war
O Lymoges! O Austria! thou dost shame
That bloody spoil:

(Shakespeare, *King John*)

The political thinker Johannes Althusius starts *Politica Methodice Digesta* by explaining his philosophical presuppositions. The term *consociato* was coined by Althusius in 1603. In *Politica Methodice Digesta* he defined *consociato* as a form of political union. Arend Lijphart, a political scientist, coined the term consociationalism, which he regarded as a kind of power-sharing. He developed a theory of consociationalism which he said had close affinities with corporatism. A consociational state is one which is divided along religious, ethnic and linguistic lines, and the theory of consociationalism has been successful in helping countries to implement power-sharing arrangements. Consociationalism democracy was successful in Switzerland, Austria, Belgium and the Netherlands but failed in Fiji, Cyprus and Lebanon.

Lijphart's four features of Consociationalism democracy:

1. A grand coalition government comes together to rule the state because they recognise the futility in not working together. All parties are represented because a wider range of views can then be considered.
2. Mutual veto: any one minority can halt proceedings and veto a policy change. Some people feared it would lead to immobility but because of the ethnic quotas the elites had too much to lose. You can have an absolute veto, a suspensive veto, a formal veto and informal veto.
3. Proportionality: decisions are to be taken out of the hands of the citizens and made by the elite in order to avoid conflict. This can mean that compromises are made behind closed doors with only the elite being privy to making judgments.
4. Segmental autonomy: minorities are to rule themselves territorially and under the federal government of the grand coalition.

In Belgium, consociationalism created territorial and non-territorial autonomy. There is Dutch-speaking Flanders and French-speaking Wallonia and French and Dutch speakers in bilingual Brussels.

In respect of the Netherlands, Brian Barry argued that 'the whole cause of the disagreement was the feeling of some Dutchman ... that it mattered what all the inhabitants of the country believed. Demands for policies aimed at producing religious or secular uniformity presuppose a concern ... for the state of grace of one's fellow citizens.' He contrasts this to the case of a society marked by conflict, in this case NI, where he argues that 'the inhabitants ... have never shown much worry about the prospects of the adherents of the other religion going to hell.'

Go back to the drawing board – the wheels have come off the wagon and the Agreement's ran out of steam.

The Agreement Written As *Finnegan's Wake*
De Moulins was seeing red. He'd puff and puff and blow her house down. Her house was made of straw. He wouldn't give her the thatch of day. She wouldn't be getting any more mollycoddles from him. No more apple crumble for her ... he wasn't going to hang around waiting for the crumbs that fell from her table. He would put on his Crombie, Passeleg would don his Crombie and they would have a big fiendonstration at the City Hall. He had friends in unflappable places. He would bring the place to a standstill. Things would get caustly. He had not seen through the Jezzybelle. He had not seen it coming. Was this the colleen who was the ultra Britberry, who was not for turning, who was not a turncoat? There was not a U-turn bone in her body. Now there she was as large as life, as plain as Napoleon's nose, signing Ulster away and not batting an eyelid or having a second thought. Sitting there like a piece of arm candy, fawning over Fils de Gilbert, the owner of the Teashop in Dovelon. It was a mad Thatcher's tea party. De Moulins could see an early grey for many. They couldn't see the earl for the grey.

She was sitting beside Geraddus Fils de Gilbert like his Darjeeling, like butter wouldn't melt on her tongue. He was fawning over her and she was toadying to him. She'd be wearing a Fáinne next. She'll be changing her name to Mairead. She has misread the situation. And she promised not to upset the status cart but now she was overturning the apple cart and he didn't like the way the cookie was crumbling. And it was not so long since some of them were in the Crum getting sentenced.

They had waited for Ceylon, they were weary of Oolonging on. But that was no reason for the Grantham lass, that Jezzybelle, to lapsang souchong along with the Greenites. He wanted her to sling her honglong over her pletco and say so long and head over the Channel. That infamous honglong was a baganal of treachery. And the province had been running like clockwork, clockwork orange. He would viddy to it that this siteaution would be sorted. She thought Jezzybelle had a mozg, but she was just a puppet, a nadmenny puppet, a manic marionette. A false Phinoccio. Did she think honest ulsteamen would accept this hen-korm? She was playing a gloopy game with ulsteamen and it would backfire. She was a blunderbuss, a bezoomny baboochka, a baddiwad eggiweg. He thought she was a blanc-blue, a true blue in a pussy-bow blouse, but now he realised she was leading them up the garden path; it looked as if tous les chemins mènent à Rome, Roman Catholicism and Dublin Castle. He was a blanc-bec for trusting her. Her stories were all bobards! She had always played with orange cards, but now she was playing Russian roulette and that bullet was reserved for the Union. She had always kept her cards on the table but now she was playing them close to her chest. We were a well-oiled machine – we marched comme sur des roulettes, like carriages on a track.

He had learned a dorogoy lesson. The Iron dama, the dama who was never for turning, was doing just that. The dama who said we will never negoteaiate with prestoopniks, not a word, not a *focal*, not a cupla of focal, not even a syllable. We will not stoop so low. She had only one song in her jukebox, 'The lady's not for turning', but now she'd cut another demo, 'The lady is a turncoat'. She didn't know her lapsang from her souchong, her dar from her jeeling. The people would hit the Ceylon. There would be periwigs on the green when this got out. She'd led them a merry jig, an rince mor, a sneaky reel, and more or less sold their birthright. The Iron dama had bad uttentions all along and now they were being forced to learn a new dance. It would be the Siege of Ennis instead of the Siege of Derry, the Walls of Limerick instead of the Walls of Derry. Hop on your heel, treble cut treble kick the heel, ship cut tip out switch feet toe up tip hop back, stamp stamp, click click … the orange is father to Christpatricus.

Sabcunsciously, and I am not boiassed, but we are catnapping into a United Earland. And they are all sitting round Hillsborrowed Castle congrandyoulikeingthemselves, playing mooseical chairs and when they all sat their beehinds down again, our chair was gone. We were oot in the cauld! They were out of control. They were out of order. We're the Orange order, we're law and order, we call the shots, we still count in this town. This whole thing is jerry built, paddypatched, ill-begotten, best forgotten, it will be verbdoden, just you wait, Maggie Swiggins, just you wait. You cry and say you're sorry, but it will be too late! Ta bron orm, Mairead, je suis termine avec vous! Je n'ai plus de sentiment d'amour pour vous. We are through.

To ami et l'ennemi to friend and foe alike je dis que nous ne serons être émus. Not an inch! Pas une pouce:

Nu un centimetru
Não uma polegada

Ne palec
Ekki tomma
Non unciae
Ní orlach
Nid mofedd

She was extending a lámh glas, a grænt hönd to the vagabonds down south. Did she know we only recognise one hand the Red Hand of Ulster the Lámh Dhearg Uladh. We are the chosen people, the people of the Covenant, the people descended from Zarah of the Red Hand who was robbed of his birthright and sent into exile.

The Agreement Written As *Hamlet*
What devil was't/That have cozen'd you at hoodman-blind?

> Ulsterious: Gertrude showed us one face, but she showed the South another. We must not let such treachery go unchecked.
> Orangious: We must be cruel to be kind. It is ill begotten and betokens even worse.
> Ulsteranious: Words, words, words!
> Orangious: There is something rotten in the province of Ulster.
> Ulsteranious: Looks like Gertie is leading us down the primrose path.
> Orangious: The time is out of kilter!
> Ulsteranious: Agreement most horrid!
> Orangious: The devil has a pleasing shape. She really took me in.
> Ulsteranious: When the wind blows southerly, I am mad north-north. I know a hawk from a dove. I know a harp from a red hand.
> Orangious: Such a rhapsody of words!
> Ulsteranious: Her signature makes oaths as empty as gamblers' pledges.
> Orangious: Infirmity, thy name is woman!
> Ulsteranious: Madness in prime ministers must not go unheeded.
> Orangious: Oh what a mighty stateswoman is now dethroned.
> Ulsteranious: Would she dare shuffle off the orange coil?
> Orangious: She has made me mad, I wish a plague on her for her perfidy.

Ulsteranious: We'll have no more agreements! The act of partition shall stand.
Orangious: A Protestant parliament for a Protestant people. We want no truck with Aras and Ucturaun.
Ulsteranious: Let her play the fool in her own house.
Orangious: She gave me a memento once!
Ulsteranious: Send it back to her!
Orangious: We will take up arms if we have to.
Ulsteranious: She thinks the Troubles are bad … but let me tell you, they are only bows and arrows compared to the wrath we will unleash.
Orangious: Our conscience will not make cowards of us.
Ulsteranious: We'll not turn back in the pith of the moment, or in the heat of the battle.
Orangious: We'll put her teeth on edge and drive our purpose home.
Ulsteranious: I am thought-sick of this mess.
Orangious: She did not even blush, slipping over the border, meeting with the Taoiseach in Áras an Uachtaráin.
Ulsteranious: We had spies in their Áras place. They hid behind the arras and heard the skulduggery. When Gordon Strong and Robert Craig returned they had a tale to tell.
Orangious: When I heard the shenanigans it was a like a thorn pricking my heart.
Ulsteranious: We will speak further on this. But mark you this, this document which was signed in madness will be burned in haste. I will tell you more anon. Act smart and pretend you do not know the gist of things to come and let secrecy 'moult no feather'. I have of late decided that we must have some method in our resistance and not give way to mayhem and madness.
Orangious: I give myself to the full bent of your command. It looks as if her loyalty to us was more honoured in the

breach than in the observance. She will rue the day she crossed us.
Ulsteranious: Her goose is cooked. Leave her to heaven!
Orangious: She has hoisted her own petard.
Ulsteranious: She may try to shape our ends, but we'll shape our destiny.

Unwilling, I agreed. Alas, too soon.
We came aboard.

(Comedy of Errors)

My Mother's Diary
Thursday, 17 September 1998

Dear Diary,
I am now in the fourth stage of the Kübler-Ross model: depression. I did not want to get up this morning. I do not want this. I cannot brace myself against the unknown. I have no guardian angel to get me through this. I am not strong enough to handle bringing up a special child on my own. I have no energy today.

The Road to Fife was Trouble and Strife

There was a sense of exuberance after the Good Friday Agreement was signed. The only thing was that it began to look like the 'Long Good Friday'. First of all the IRA took cold feet about decommissioning; some members said that the Agreement was a compromise and a sell-out and they formed a dissident group called the Real IRA. However, 71% of people in Northern Ireland voted in favour of the Agreement at the 22 May 1998 referendum. In total 676,966 people voted for the Agreement and 274,979 voted against it. The turnout in the North was 81.1%. In the South citizens had to vote on a change to their constitution. The amendment allowed the state to comply with the Good Friday Agreement and removed the South's territorial claim on the North. 1,442,583 people voted in favour and 85,748 said no. The turnout was 56.3%.

The first elections of politicians to the Northern Ireland Assembly were held on 25 June 1998 but the forced marriage was already fraying at the edges. The IRA were not going to decommission until they saw the prison gates opening and the republican prisoners being released. They also wanted the military to be scaled-down and the RUC reformed. Meanwhile the stand-off at Drumcree was in full flow. To quote Sean O'Casey's Captain Boyle, 'Th' whole worl's in a terrible state o' chassis'. The Northern Ireland Assembly had the lifespan of a mayfly. After it was elected in June 1998, it had its inaugural meeting on 1 July 1998, but full powers were not devolved until December 1999. It was like a toy given to a child to play with but if the child didn't look after the toy, it would be taken away. Brendan Behan once said that 'the first item on the agenda of any new Irish organisation was the split'. Decommissioning was not happening fast enough for Trimble and he threatened to resign. After many more meetings and behind-the-scenes dealing, the Assembly was back again in May 2000. It had a short lease of life and was suspended again on 10 August 2001, but this was only a twenty-four-hour suspension. It was once again suspended on 22 September, again for twenty-four hours. It was then suspended again, like an unruly schoolboy, but this time the boy was practically sent down as the suspension lasted from 14 October 2002–7 May 2007. It was a comedy of errors and reminds me of the ZZ Ward song 'Put the Gun Down'.

The road to decommissioning was paved with good intentions. The UVF wanted to put their arms beyond reach but Gusty Spence, who founded the group in 1966, said that placing the guns beyond reach did not equate to the full decommissioning of arms; it didn't satisfy the decommissioning criteria as defined by De Chastelain.

This is a transcript detailing the decommissioning process which I shall call 'We cannot say':

Peter Weir (North Down Ulster Unionist Assembly member): Do you have a full inventory from the IRA of all their weapons?

Gen de Chastelain: They have not given us one. We have no figures from any of the paramilitary groups. We have been given what security sources, the RUC, Army and Garda believe the IRA hold. We have asked for these estimates to be updated in light of seizures, etc., but we are working with security force figures. Jane's Defence Manual also has estimates. The various estimates do agree.

Peter Weir: Did the decommissioning take place at one site or in more than one place?

Gen de Chastelain: We were asked a similar question by the DUP and I can say again that there was one event and you can read the answer from that.

Peter Weir: How did you travel to the site where decommissioning took place?

Gen de Chastelain: We don't propose to detail methods here. I did not travel by helicopter or by sea. I was on the island of Ireland but I do not know exactly where. I could have got there by car, by bicycle or I could have walked.

Peter Weir: Was any inventory taken of the number of arms destroyed?

Gen de Chastelain: An inventory was taken at the event. This was required by the scheme and regulations. It took account of all the items put beyond use.

Peter Weir: How many of the Commissioners were present?

Gen de Chastelain: The three Commissioners were present. There were no support staff present.

Peter Weir: Was the IRA representative to the IICD present at the decommissioning event?

Gen de Chastelain: I did allow that this was the case. One representative was there – we have been dealing with the same individual throughout. I cannot say how many people were there in total.

Peter Weir: You were in Canada in the days before decommissioning. When did you return to Northern Ireland?

Gen de Chastelain: I left on Tuesday or Wednesday and I came back last Sunday. We reported on Tuesday that the event took place. We report events as soon as we can.

Peter Weir: Did the event take place on Monday?

Gen de Chastelain: We report events as soon as we can.

William Ross (Former East Londonderry MP): Were the guns, explosives, etc. inside a structure?

Gen de Chastelain: We do not want to get into discussing methods. They were produced, we took an inventory and they were put beyond use.

William Ross: Were they in good condition?

Gen de Chastelain: We felt that the weapons, ammunition and explosives were operational.

William Ross: Were they greased?

Gen de Chastelain: I am not saying. They were not beyond use already.

William Ross: Was an inventory of the types of weapons, models, etc. taken?

Gen de Chastelain: We took an inventory of the number of weapons put beyond use. We did not take one of the serial numbers. We knew what type of weapons they were from our own knowledge.

William Ross: Could you have fired the weapons?

Gen de Chastelain: They were operational. We handled them.

William Ross: Were the weapons used in the past?

Gen de Chastelain: We cannot say.

William Ross: The ammunition – were you able to count it?

Gen de Chastelain: We were able to examine it, count it and then watch it be put beyond use.

William Ross: If there were a large number of rounds then it would need to be boxed? Were there boxes?

Gen de Chastelain: We cannot say.

William Ross: Were you able to identify various calibres of ammunition?

Gen de Chastelain: We recognised what calibre the ammunition was.

William Ross: Were you able to identify what explosives were there?

Gen de Chastelain: We spent time with the RUC and security forces examining different weapons and materials used by paramilitaries, so we know what to look for.

William Ross: Was there any commercial explosive, what we would know as gelignite?

Gen de Chastelain: We do not want to go into details. The explosives were what they purported to be and the quantities also. We reported that.

William Ross: Were there any mortars or any weapons that could have been of terrorist manufacture?

Gen de Chastelain: What we saw here came under what I as a soldier would class as a weapon.

William Ross: Were the weapons buried in concrete?

Gen de Chastelain: We have heard various reports and we have not speculated on any of these.

William Ross: It has been reported that acid may have been added to the concrete to help corrode the weapons. However, concrete is an alkaline substance and the addition of acid could make it weak. Surely this would lead to problems?

Gen de Chastelain: I would say that we felt that at the end of the event, it had met its remits.

William Ross: Would the covering of weapons by concrete alone meet the remits of decommissioning?

Gen de Chastelain: Our remit is that decommissioning means weapons put permanently inaccessible or permanently unusable. It met those.

William Ross: If concrete were used, would you be able to determine the strength of the concrete mix used?

Gen de Chastelain: Any answer to this would determine that this was the method used, so I cannot reply to that.

William Ross: How long were you present at the site for?

Gen de Chastelain: A matter of hours. I am not going to go into how many. Days are a matter of hours. Months are a matter of hours.

William Ross: Would it have been five or six?

Gen de Chastelain: I will not specify.

William Ross: The best way to dispose of explosives would be either to reduce it with acid, detonate it or to burn it. It is obvious that none of these was used?

Gen de Chastelain: We are required to make sure what is done is safe and it was safe in this case.

Peter King (anti-Good Friday Agreement Ulster Unionist): The regulations governing decommissioning have been extended. Does this imply that the methods used would not have fulfilled the initial criteria?

Gen de Chastelain: The first scheme had two main methods: either giving information which would lead to the discovery and so destruction of weapons or the handing over of weapons for destruction. The second scheme allows other methods to be used. The only change, however, other than the increase in the use of phrases 'permanently inaccessible and permanently unusable' was the inclusion of a paragraph where we could use other methods which still meet the requirements.

Pauline Armitage (East Londonderry Ulster Unionist Assembly member): Did you finally decide on the disposal method?

Gen de Chastelain: The disposal methods used are decided with the individual paramilitary groups. We have a conditional agreement with the UVF (loyalist Ulster Volunteer Force) and the UFF (loyalist Ulster Freedom Fighters). The paramilitary groups have to agree to decommission and we have to agree that the method meets regulations. There was an announcement on the 5th or 6th of August that we agreed a method by which arms could be put beyond use.

Pauline Armitage: Do you think the public should know what happened?

Gen de Chastelain: We would prefer it if everything was done openly. The paramilitary group decided that it would not be made public in the same way that the LVF (Loyalist Volunteer Force) decided that their act of decommissioning would be made public. Everyone would like to see weapons cut up into confetti. Since it is a voluntary process, then to succeed certain things should apply. One of these was that whatever method is used should not signify surrender or defeat of that group.

Pauline Armitage: Why can you not release exactly what was decommissioned?

Gen de Chastelain: That is part of the same situation. We do have an inventory which will be presented to the two Governments after all the events of decommissioning have occurred. It could also be presented to them earlier if requested. What they do with it then is up to them.

Pauline Armitage: Would the Prime Minister like to know what has been decommissioned?

Gen de Chastelain: That is up to him.

Pauline Armitage: Are you dictated to by the IRA regarding meetings, etc., and exactly what goes on?

Gen de Chastelain: Only when the meetings will take place.

Pauline Armitage: If there were two or three decommissioning events a year, how long would it take for total decommissioning to be completed?

Gen de Chastelain: I cannot say; any event of decommissioning could include large amounts or it could include smaller amounts.

Pauline Armitage: Based on what was done last week, if there were two or three events per year, how long would it take?

Gen de Chastelain: If I answered that directly, then I would be talking about quantities and I cannot do that.

Pauline Armitage: Would it take 10 months or 10 years?

Gen de Chastelain: If I answered that, you could determine what weapons the IRA has and make estimates as to quantities put beyond use.

Pauline Armitage: It has been suggested that it could take 20 years.

Gen de Chastelain: I have heard suggestions of 20 years, two years, that there were two dumps or three dumps. We are not confirming or denying anything.
William Ross: Will the Government not get the complete inventory until decommissioning has been completed?
Gen de Chastelain: They could ask for it earlier.
Pauline Armitage: If there are regular decommissioning events, could decommissioning be completed by February 2002?
Gen de Chastelain: If it came in large amounts over a period of days, then we could be completed long before that. We have always felt that two months was an adequate amount of time. If we are working to a target, when we approach the point when we cannot meet it, we would approach Government and tell them.
Peter Weir: Is it the case that it is the Government's choice as to whether any inventory would be made public?
Gen de Chastelain: We recommended to the Government and the parties in 1998 that if decommissioning was to succeed, then there might be circumstances where confidentiality would need to apply. That was the recommendation of the IICD to the Government and parties.
Peter Weir: Does the ultimate decision about making it public lie with the Government?
Gen de Chastelain: If we give them the information, then yes. We do not have to give them the information.
Pauline Armitage: Do you have a programme laid out with the IRA to continue decommissioning?
Gen de Chastelain: No we don't. We have a system of meeting with the IRA. We arrange to get together. Normally, we report on these meetings to the two Governments. We don't make public what goes on. We have been meeting more frequently over the last few months.

Pauline Armitage: Do they contact you or do you contact the IRA?
Gen de Chastelain: Normally, they contact us. We have arranged to meet with the representative again soon.
William Ross: Do you know when the meeting will be, though?
Gen de Chastelain: We do not know. It will be soon but we don't know the exact date.
William Ross: Going back to the place where decommissioning took place. Have you an idea where you were?
Gen de Chastelain: We knew approximately where we were but not exactly.
William Ross: Were you in the United Kingdom?
Gen de Chastelain: I do not know whether I was in the UK or not. I can say though that we were on the island of Ireland.

There is a lot more to this interview but I have only picked the parts relevant to this book. I would like to look at de Chastelain's reply to one of Peter Weir's questions more closely. Obviously the location of the decommissioning site was in Ireland as he did not travel by helicopter or by sea (although there's nothing to say you can't travel across land in a helicopter.

He says he didn't know where he was. He said he could have travelled there by car, bicycle or could have walked. Would it seem credible that a man of General de Chastelain's pedigree would just hop on a bike and cycle to a decommissioning site? Alfred John Gardyne Drummond de Chastelain was born in 1937. He served twice as Canada's Chief of the Defence Staff and became head of the Independent International Commission on Decommissioning in NI. He does not strike me as the happy-go-lucky type who would present himself at an IRA arms cache on a bicycle. Nor can I see a man of his importance walking to his destination – yet he could have walked. Technically anyone could walk to a meeting. You could walk from Malin Head, the most northerly tip of Ireland, to Mizen Head in the south if you had the time and the right walking shoes. I think the general travelled by car because he would have needed some kind of handler or minder to take him to the site; he may well have been blindfolded. As he was a military man I'm sure he wasn't unduly stressed about being escorted to an unknown destination, and as a military man he would have had the expertise to know what it meant to put weaponry beyond use.

His reply to William Ross's question about the length of time he spent at the site was indeed puzzling:

> A matter of hours. I am not going to go into how many. Days are a matter of hours. Months are a matter of hours.

Logically a day is made up of hours and months are made up of days, and so forth. Was William Ross trying to determine the amount of weaponry vis-à-vis the length of time at the making of the inventory and the decommissioning of the weapons? William Ross also made a very interesting point about the decommissioning process:

> … concrete is an alkaline substance and the addition of acid could make it weak. Surely this would lead to problems?

I do so wish the general had answered this question.

My Mother's Diary
Friday, 18 September 1998

Dear Diary,
I cannot say I will ever reach the fifth stage of the model: acceptance. I do not want this, Patrick does not deserve this and neither of us accept this.

I will now investigate the debates that have taken place in Stormont. A lot of important people invested a lot of time and money in getting the folk on the hill to agree to sit together under one roof. I will write this in a Christopher-John-Francis-Boone voice as he is a young boy (although fictional) who describes himself as 'a mathematician with some behavioural difficulties'. Occasionally I ask myself what Christopher would do next. I would like to see if they are telling the truth up there on the hill and if they really have buried the hatchet (although normally speaking I do not like metaphors, in this case it is justified). Yes, I think maybe an approach similar to *The Curious Incident of the Dog in the Night-Time* would be beneficial in carrying out an appraisal of the newly devolved Assembly. The first item I looked at was the minutes of the first meeting of the Assembly Commission held on 17 May 2007 at 10.30am in room 106. These were some of the items discussed:

> 7.1.5 The British/Irish Council – Speaker drew Members' attention to a paper containing information about a British/Irish summit.
> 7.1.6 Business Cards for MLAs – Mr Evans to investigate the delay in the availability of ivory business cards for MLAs.
> 7.1.7 Sound System and Heating in Parliament Buildings – Members raised the issue of poor acoustics within the Chamber during plenary sittings. The issue of heating was also raised. Mr Evans agreed to investigate both issues and come back to an early Commission meeting with proposals.

I hope I am not being petty, but I wonder why the MLAs would want ivory business cards. Are elephants not an endangered species? And what about the illegal trade in tiger bone, bear bile, rhino horn and Tibetan Shahtoosh shawls? Where will it all end? Will they all want ivory carvings in their offices? Is it all about status symbols? Ivory-plated mobile phones, rhino-horned ornaments?

I also looked at the minutes of 21 June 2007 which related to the audio system in the chamber:

> Mr Evans spoke to a paper on the acoustic difficulties experienced by Members in the Assembly Chamber and recommended the upgrading of equipment during the Summer Recess. Members agreed that work should be carried out to the microphones and asked that the Business Committee be advised about the arrangements.

I know these details are important. But that is what they are – *details*. Surely someone could be appointed to look after the tech side of things. I am wondering if we aren't able to see past the end of our noses, getting a little bit wood for the trees and too big for our boots!

When I read the item concerning the commissioning of the former First and Deputy First Minister which was raised by the Rev Coulter on 20 September 2007:

> Rev Coulter raised the issue of commissioning portraits of the former First and Deputy First Minister. It was agreed, in principle, that this should be taken forward. Mr Logue to explore this matter.

Commissioning paintings! Does that involve a tendering process? Do the artists have to come to an interview?

I did laugh at this entry from 4 October 2007:

> 4.5 The Speaker asked Ms McClelland to investigate the waiting times for food in the Members Dining Room.

Waiting times for MLAs in the members' dining room! Are we getting a bit precious here? At the same time, I know waiting can be a chore. I remember how Claire, my teaching assistant, had to support me in queuing up for my lunchtime meal in the school canteen. The first time she took me she put me at a table near the door. I hated the way they shoved the food on your plate. The carrots were over boiled and didn't taste like carrots, more like cardboard. I begged my mother to let me take my lunch with me so I could eat it in the classroom. But, no, Mother said, 'It would be better for you to eat with your classmates.' She's in denial about my condition and thinks that a mainstream education is a cure-all for autism.

I hated queues so much. On some occasions we had to wait five minutes and the children would become noisy and boisterous. I felt uncomfortable. They behaved like that in the playground, only worse. Their games seemed like a form of horseplay: the boys would scrap and try to push one another to the ground while the girls would gather in little huddles and whisper a lot of nonsense. Some of them had silly Alice bands in their hair.

On 18 October 2007:

> Mr Moutray raised a number of issues. Firstly he expressed his concern at the amount of rubbish and debris in the upper west car park area. He also raised the issue of poor lighting in the lower east car park and the quality of the replacement table in room 21. Additionally issues were raised about the number of guests using the basement restaurant/members facilities during sitting days. The Speaker confirmed that he had written to a Member with regard to this issue.

I have to say that I had no idea that MLAs spent time on the particulars of rubbish, poor lighting in the car park and office furniture.

Mr Butler also expressed concerns about 'unsolicited approaches to Ministers and MLAs within Parliament Buildings'. Then Mr Logue 'confirmed that there were protocols in place, agreed by the previous Commission. He agreed to re-visit these protocols and bring them [up] at a future Commission meeting.' He then 'raised the issue of poor quality of existing photocopying equipment and suggested that it might be appropriate to review this provision'.

At last I stumbled upon something which inspired me to think that I might be able to put on my *Curious Incident of the Dog in the Night-Time* hat:

> Mr Maginness informed the Commission that the Minister for Social Development, Margaret Ritchie, would be writing to the Commission in connection with an incident which had occurred in Parliament Buildings.

Now that is real 'Curious Incident' speak! I could use some of Christopher's forensic skills here. Mr Butler mentioned 'unsolicited approaches to Ministers and MLAs within Parliament Buildings'. Was this the kind of incident Margaret Ritchie would be writing about?

The Oxford Dictionary defines he word 'incident' as 'an instance of something happening; an event or occurrence'. The event can be an amusing one or a violent clash between two parties. The word's etymology is defined as:

> Late Middle English: via Old French from Latin *incident-* 'falling upon, happening to', from the verb *incidere*, from *in-* 'upon' and *cadere* 'to fall'.

I suppose being an MLA is just like being at school – you have to obey the rules. There is a code of conduct which they all have to sign up to. Unlike school there are no parents to appeal to if an incident arises. But the code gives clarity around behaviour nonetheless.

The Code of Conduct of the Northern Ireland Assembly

Selflessness
Integrity
Objectivity
Accountability
Openness
Honesty
Leadership
Equality
Promoting Good Relations
Respect
Good Working Relationships

And if any of the MLAs are in doubt, there is a Clerk of Standards who 'if necessary, will seek adjudication from the Committee on Standards and Privileges'.

I suppose Parliament Buildings is like a school: in a school little events or incidents are magnified out of all proportion. For example, not wearing the correct uniform – that could spark off a major incident. You might even finish up having to report to the headmaster's office. You would get a dressing-down for not dressing correctly. Being late for class could draw down the wrath of the gods. There would be a big outcry if you used bad language in the class. For example, if you told the teacher to 'fuck off', that would be an incident. You might become the class hero and get kudos for being the class clown, but, as regards the teachers, you are a marked man. So for the first eighteen years of our lives we are subject to rules for our behaviour that are embedded in the school code of conduct. University has rules as well, but they are not as obvious. Those rules are to attend lectures, seminars, do our essays and then complete our undergraduate studies and choose a career. Imagine, some people choose to become teachers and after a few years return to an environment of rules and regulations.

Well, the Assembly is like a glorified school only, and maybe I should say unfortunately, there are no pupils, so everybody is more or less on a par. Therefore everyone wants to be the teacher or the person at the top of the class doing all the talking, and this means that a major incident is probably happening during every debate as no one is really in charge. It would seem that the Speaker is in charge:

> The chief characteristics of the office of Speaker are authority and impartiality. In debates, all speeches are addressed to the Speaker and his choice of Members to speak is not open to dispute.
> (NI Assembly Website)

David Hencke, an English political journalist, referred to Prime Minister's Questions as being 'a bear garden' and that the Speaker needed to keep a rein on the proceedings:

> His role is like a strict disciplinarian headmaster trying to control overgrown adolescents shouting down and jeering their opponents like kids in a school playground.

In fact, some of the MLAs were teachers before they became politicians. Sammy Wilson, DUP, taught at Grosvenor Grammar School and became head of economics. He was also assistant chief examiner at CCEA, the examination board for Northern Ireland. Michelle McIlveen, DUP, taught at Grosvenor Grammar School as well. Both Sammy Wilson and Michelle McIlveen taught Stephen Agnew of the Green Party.

> Mr Agnew once said in a newspaper interview that he sits in the 'naughty corner' in the assembly – a reference to his

position on the backbenches with parties such as the TUV and UKIP.

Diane Dodds, DUP, taught history and English in Laurelhill Community College, Lisburn. John Hume, SDLP, architect of the Northern Ireland peace process and Nobel Peace Prize winner qualified as a French and history teacher.

Even the name 'Assembly' suggests school: a place where there is an assembly held every day. A school assembly has been defined as 'a gathering of all or part of a school in order to communicate information and share learning experiences'.

In school the teacher calls the roll and you have to affirm your presence. Paul Muldoon wrote a poem about calling the roll in two different contexts. He called it *Anseo* – the Irish for here or present. At the Collegelands Primary School a young boy, Joseph Mary Plunkett Ward, is often absent from school and is caned by the stern headmaster on his return.

So no matter what their role was before the end of hostilities, usually the elected politicians came from some kind of training background, whether legal or illegal. It is not surprising, therefore, that an institutional air pervades the Assembly chamber.

By the time the Assembly was a reality, or a quasi-reality, and free from quick fixes and peremptory suspensions, I was in a mainstream classroom and I had a teaching assistant called Claire. Claire was plunked down beside me for most of the day; she was like my shadow. At the beginning I was reluctant to have her beside me, but, when I realised I had no choice, I decided I had to make the best of it. There was a child in the class with ADHD and she had responsibility for him as well. She was a psychology graduate who wanted to become an educational psychologist. Claire knew I had trouble blocking out noise sometimes and that I lose my concentration easily, so she prepared laminates for me so that I understood the lessons. I do not like the texture of the laminate.

Sometimes the teacher's voice was hoarse. She always seemed to have a cold. She was a rather untidy woman and her clothes came straight out of Noah's ark.

Her words were so transient. They sort of floated out and dissolved into thin air. And the other pupils started talking and carrying on. Our teacher, Miss Logan, put us at different tables according to our abilities. I was stuck with Teddy who suffers from ADHD and is so annoying – always swinging off his chair and tapping his foot. It's infuriating. Teddy has as much personality as a stuffed rabbit. There are two other boys at the table and one girl. The two boys seem to have some kind of learning impairment. They are definitely on the spectrum and they seem to exist on chicken nuggets and chips. The girl will only eat waffles and pancakes.

My experiences of school assembly were almost as traumatic as the first meetings of the new Northern Ireland Assembly. I hated having to undergo this event each morning, and I wondered why anyone had invented such a ritual.

I had to cover my ears. There were just too many rows of children shuffling and pushing, being corralled into the big hall, addressed by the school principal and then being shepherded out again. It seemed a huge waste of time and it never got any easier. I coped by placing my hands over my ears and pretending I was in my bedroom at home. How could the other children not be annoyed? They seemed to take it all in their stride.

In the nursery my teaching assistant had made me an emotional thermometer which helped me from becoming too overwhelmed. I would point at the thermometer when I was feeling stressed and needed time out. Now I was in a sea of chaos without an anchor.

In a way, some members of the new Assembly behaved as if they had autism. They couldn't adjust to the new situation. Some demonstrated poor social skills while some talked really loudly, as if they were the only people in the world. Also, their behaviour was characterised as repetitive and stereotyped. Some of them had difficulty making eye contact, some were unable to understand the rules of conversation, others didn't want physical contact. Some moved too close to the people they were talking to – invading their personal space. Some had obsessive ideas and wanted to repeat the same story over and over again, some had an impairment of social imagination and a deficiency in social interaction. For example, one side's war cry had been, 'We will never go into government with terrorists'. Suddenly they had to develop a new mindset and this tested their creativity – now sitting down at the table and starting to act as politicians stressed them out. So instead of stop-and-search the province was treated to a stop-go-stop process of devolved government. Just as I found it difficult to follow lessons because of sensory overload, so too some of the politicians found it difficult to focus on the realities of the departments of agriculture, economic development, education and finance because they were distracted by unfinished business, unresolved issues, wounds that had not healed, un-decommissioned guns that had not been put beyond use, unsolved killings, unspeakable crimes and some things that had not gone away. The only difference was that my disability had been diagnosed, and, to an extent, my new school was offering me support and addressing my needs. The Assembly members were deemed to be mentally stable human beings free from any impairment, and this may well have been the case, but having to power share was a step too far for some of them.

I never seemed to get the gist of things as I concentrated too much on the details. I then had sensory overload, was unable to process so much data and found it difficult to follow a lesson. My teaching assistant helped me to focus but sometimes I drifted off. One day the teacher was reading a story about Hans Brinker, a little Dutch boy who was supposed to have saved the town by placing his finger in a hole in the dyke. I liked that story. I think I could save the Agreement, but my savant skills have taken a nosedive since I started primary school. In the nursery all the children were basically like innocuous monkeys who only wanted to play in the sandpit and chase each other around the playground. And my mother's proximity gave me a safety net when I attended nursery. Once I started the primary school, however, I felt like Milton's Eve in *Paradise Lost* who said:

> O unexpected stroke, worse than of Death!
> Must I leave thee, Paradise? Thus leave
> Thee, native soil? These happy walks and shades.

I felt it was a kind of banishment, a cruel expulsion. In the nursery I was allowed to have my own little rules and rituals and I felt secure. There were far too many people at the primary school. The rallying call these days is mainstreaming. All these neurotic mothers whose mantra is, 'I want my child educated at a mainstream school'. Do they not realise that for an autistic child mainstreaming is a minefield, and that there are many unexploded devices waiting to trip us up?

The Limbo Years

Limbo is the place where the souls of the unbaptised were banished and can also be defined as 'an uncertain period of awaiting a decision or resolution'. When the Assembly was in limbo work went on behind the scenes to get it up and running again. Who wants to be ruled by peripatetic ministers from Westminster? There were accusations made that the suspension of the Assembly and the re-institution of direct rule suited the Unionists as it meant the end of a forced power-sharing.

Eddie McGrady said the DUP were in denial. He complained about the DUP's negative attitude towards power-sharing and that behind closed doors they were undermining the NI Assembly as they would have been only too glad if direct rule was reinstated:

> Get rid of David Trimble!
> You did it before.
> You did it with Terence O'Neill.
> You did it with Chichester-Clark.
> You did it with Brian Faulkner.

The Hansard (the official record of the NI Assembly proceedings) for 9 October 2000 read like an acrimonious gathering of politicians garnered from two opposing sides, and rather than power-sharing it was more like power splitting. There is a framework which was formulated by Bruce Tuckman to describe the phases of development groups go through, namely Forming, Storming, Norming, Performing and Adjourning. Every team or group needs to go through these stages in order to deal with issues and to deliver results. After reading the Hansard record for that day, I can conclude that in the new millennium the Assembly power struggles impeded any kind of constructive government. Eddie McGrady was waging a verbal war on the DUP who was waging war on David Trimble who had signed the Good Friday Agreement, and the SDLP were at odds with Sinn Féin and so on and so forth. Seamus Close of the Alliance Party also castigated the DUP for their litany of 'goes':

> We then moved on to Secretaries of State.
> Willy Whitelaw had to go, Merlyn Rees had to go,
> Mo Mowlam had to go — they all had to go.
> Even Governors of Northern Ireland
> suffered the same fate; they were told to go.
> Moderators of the church were told to go,
> not to mention His Holiness the Pope.
> Anybody who tried to bring about change in
> Northern Ireland was told by the party on my left,
> the party of political shenanigans,
> to pack their bags and go.

The language from one of the members, Alex Atwood, a SDLP MLA, in the Hansard from 20 March 2007 reflected the mood of his party. He acknowledged that there had been a reduction in 'binding and shackling Ministers and putting Ministers and Government into a straitjacket', but he still feared that the Pledge of Office would create the possibility that members could face legal action. He said 'if that does not put a straitjacket on Members, I do not know what does', and near the end of the speech he urged an amendment because the pledge created a 'straitjacket round the Assembly and the Executive'.

Peter Robinson, DUP, responded to Attwood's remarks in a sarcastic way. He said, 'I had not intended to speak, until I heard the Member's remarks. Today has just got longer.' This phrase references time and gives the impression that time has begun to drag. He also refers to the meeting as being mind-numbingly long-winded.

He undermines Attwood's legal qualifications (he has a law degree from Queen's University) by remarking, 'I had thought that he had something of a legal background.' He also referred to the necessity to have a ministerial Pledge of Office in an Assembly 'where, quite frankly, there is not the level of trust that allows normal conventions to operate'. He concludes his remarks by suggesting that Attwood should 'save it [his breath] for blowing his porridge in the morning'.

I did not find these interchanges very empowering. They suggest that there were many unpalatable planks of history that were continually resurfacing.

The next person to speak in the meeting was Sinn Féin's Conor Murphy. Sinn Féin promotes the use of the Irish language and his opening remarks were in Irish: 'Go raibh maith agat, a Cheann Comhairle.' He refers to the SDLP's 'sound bites' and 'drive-by vetoes' and finished by commenting, 'whatever that meant was lost on almost everyone else.'

No unanimity so far! Ian Paisley commented, 'I do not know what is wrong with this House today. There have been difficulties with the recording machines, and there is a clock that does not know whether it is working. There is also a breath of what I call "stepmother's air" in this Building today.'

Paisley's comments, like Robinson's, also reference time. However Robinson's words suggest that he feels the process is being drawn-out, and he indicates that he is feeling overburdened by Attwood's opinions. Paisley's words have a certain Gestalt tinge to them – he suggested that the 'time is out of joint'; the clock and the recording equipment were not working correctly and they represent the way the Assembly members were out of joint with each other.

In Gestalt psychology the whole is more than the sum of the parts. By drawing the group's attention to the behaviour of the clock, to the stifling feeling of the air, Paisley was bringing the group away from their projections by putting them in touch with the ambience of the chamber.

The online Oxford Dictionary defines phenomenology as 'the science of phenomena as distinct from that of the nature of being', and also 'an approach that concentrates on the study of consciousness and the objects of direct experience'. In the context of Gestalt therapy, phenomenology is a process where the therapist and the client engage in direct awareness rather than digging into the past in a Freudian sense or offering Rogerian unconditional positive regard. The only time a trip down memory lane is taken is when a client is stuck in a fixed gestalt because in Gestalt therapy awareness perception and feelings in the present are more important than explanations and rationalisations. The main aim of the therapy is to become aware of what is happening in the here and now.

In terms of the group's dynamics, the MLAs were carrying issues from the past and dragging them into the present. Ian Paisley was right to call the group's attention to the present moment. He was hoping to dismiss the malign breath of the wicked stepmother whose evil perverted the course of justice in many a Disney or Brothers Grimm fairy tale. Could Ian Paisley have been correct in his analysis of the atmosphere in the House?

Joseph Zinker said that a group was an organism in its own right:

> The group is a living, organic entity. It is larger than the sum of individuals in it. That large figure, that organism, is in process, constantly changing. Aside from its initial scattered quality and subsequent cohesiveness, the group transforms itself: its colour, its playfulness, its mourning, its sense of contact, as well as its deflections, may stand out at any given moment of its life.

The tragedy was that the more moderate parties, the SDLP and the Ulster Unionist Party, were losing ground to the more extreme parties, Sinn Féin and the DUP. Having these two diametrically opposed parties in close proximity was certainly going to raise the tension. These two parties, who were more at home with mud-slinging, were now being asked to function in a power-sharing Assembly which was established to run the province. Carrying out the day-to-day functions of government meant that the 108 MLAs would have to find common ground and let go of past grievances in order to deal with the exigencies and bread-and-butter issues of the present. Instead of the fairy-tale ending, the atmosphere was at times contaminated with whataboutery, which happens when people are feeling challenged or threatened; they retreat into their tribal position and project blame onto their perceived rivals. Harking back to the past would have held no water with Fritz Perls; he wouldn't agree with people staying stuck in their undigested gestalts.

> Perls had no time for tracing back associations to some dubious infantile trauma, but concentrated, like Jung, on discovering buried treasure within the personality. He focused his attention on actual behaviour in a group situation – facial expression, tone of voice, posture, gesture, reactions to other members, and so on – in order to discover the holes in a person's present personality.

It was not conducive to furthering the aims of the power-sharing Assembly. Too many of the parties were harking back to the past, and too many were mired in their fixed gestalts. In a way it had all the potential to be a shining example of how two warring communities could forsake violence and turn their swords into ploughshares, their spears into pruning forks. However, the swords were turned into cross words and childish jibes, and the fairy dust was soon blowing off the fairy-tale ending. For the most part the violence had ended and the Troubles were over. There had been a lot of horse-trading, stunts and stand-offs since the Agreement was signed in 1998. A lot of long days and nights of negotiations and compromises and broken promises had been made on the journey from guns to government, but finally Northern Ireland had its own devolved Assembly. Unfortunately the fairy-tale ending is never guaranteed. At any moment a ghost from the past could stare through the glass; a cold icy blast from the past could rock the very foundations of the nascent Assembly. Would it be possible to power-share with so much unfinished business, so many unanswered questions? The Troubles were over but a new war was beginning, a war of words. And from the Hansard report everyone had the gift of the gab and everyone had a *kist o wurds*, but no one seemed to have any answers.

There was a feeling that the timing of the Agreement was not right. Roy Beggs Jnr from the Ulster Unionist Party indicated that the devolution of policing and justice was a step too far. He commented that:

> The Ulster Unionist Party does not believe that the Assembly is ready for the devolution of policing and justice or that it should debate such divisive issues, as that could have a destabilising effect. The unionist community is not ready for the devolution of those powers.

Aristotle said that 'nature abhors a vacuum', and a sample of the Hansard report eighteen months later, on 15 September 2008, demonstrates this very point. Dolores Kelly referred to the rise in dissident violence. She pointed out that the dissidents were taking advantage of the political vacuum and filling it with rioting and violence. She laid the blame for the vacuum at the door of Sinn Féin and the DUP, whom she accused of indulging in 'selfish party brinkmanship and standoffs'. She called for leadership and for the last piece of the jigsaw to be completed. It was as if Maleficent, the bad fairy, had withheld the last piece and refused to let the puzzle be completed – *The Myth of Sisyphus* with an Ulster theme.

The Troubles lurked like a great white shark in between ministers trying to agree the second stage of the Disease of Animals Bill and discussing measures to protect the mobile library service. David Simpson, MLA, brought up a recent spate of attacks by dissidents throughout the province, and like an unwanted Banquo at the feast, the past kept raising its ugly head.

One minute the Hansard was recording the minutiae of everyday running of the government: the bills, the possibility of giving an aid package to the farmers who had lost crops in the recent flooding, scoping exercises on dog control and dangerous dogs legislation (the pros and cons of banning different breeds), farm modernisation plans and so forth, and the next minute the Troubles raised its head. When raising the issue of republican dissident activity, David Simpson's speak went into oratorical overdrive and he used rhetorical questions and repetition to hammer his point home. Three sentences in his speech were prefaced with, 'Do they really think …' or 'Do they really believe …'. He then launched into a diatribe about the sectarian slaughter of the Provos. This seemed to me not to be relevant to the discussion and not in the interests of promoting cross-party agreement.

> The time is out of joint; O cursed spite
> That I was ever born to set it right!

On 16 June 2009, John O'Dowd from Sinn Féin commented that, 'The person to whom I looked for advice on budgetary control was my mother, who reared nine of us on a very limited budget.' He then gave a lengthy talk interspersed with phrases like, 'they [the British government] have a debt to this society that will be paid out over many years' and 'we are not isolationists and we do not seek to cut ourselves off and float into the middle of the Atlantic' and 'we must ensure that we have an equality-driven agenda that focuses on targeting social needs, so that we can improve society'. He also said, 'We have a vision of an Ireland of equals, in which we can work and co-operate with our nearest neighbours in England, Scotland and Wales, take our place as equals in the greater European framework' and ended by commenting, 'If we are to improve our economic lot, we will have to listen to and learn from each other. That is the only way forward for society.' He signed off in Irish: 'Go raibh maith agat, a LeasCheann Comhairle.'

Peter Weir, DUP, said in response to John O'Dowd that he had a sense of déjà vu. He then made an ironic statement in order to undermine him:

> However, it is difficult for me to follow a speech that I think is almost worthy of a Nobel Prize in economics. Sinn Féin's analysis of the economy shows that that party would have difficulty distinguishing between Milton Friedman and Milton Keynes.

He spoke about the 'old hobby horses ridden round the paddock'. He pooh-poohed the idea of looking southward and hinted that to 'embrace de Valera' would be the kiss of death. He ended his speech saying he regretted the absence of David McNarry (who had been expelled from the debate by the Speaker for unparliamentary comments) and said his absence 'is almost like *Hamlet* without the prince'. Hamlet is plagued so much by his conscience that he delays killing his stepfather.

> And thus the native hue of resolution
> Is sicklied o'er with the pale cast of thought,
> And enterprises of great pitch and moment,
> With this regard their currents turn awry.
> And lose the name of action.

Selling Shellfish

Michelle Gildernew's speech was the most colourful. She was the then Minister of Agriculture and Rural Development. She spoke on illegal fishing:

> Illegal fishing activity also undermines the market for crabs and lobsters … the regulations placed a pot limit for recreational fishing of up to five pots per person, and landing limits of one lobster and five crabs per day … Just last month, 17 pots were seized and retained near Dunseverick, and 24 lobsters and 30 brown crabs were released from those pots back into the sea. Included in the seizure was one stock box containing 12 lobsters alone. Last month, 36 pots were also seized around Rathlin Island: 24 lobsters and 74 brown crabs were released … It is interesting to note that the 87 pots seized by inspectors since last autumn contained 52 lobsters and 116 crabs. That is an average of over one lobster for every two pots and just over one crab per pot … David Hilditch asked about stock boxes. A stock pot is an essential requirement for people who fish commercially and who set a large number of pots to land a marketable quantity of fresh crab and lobster.

On 30 June 2009, Health Minister Michael McGimpsey said this in the House in relation to health precautions during the Swine Flu epidemic scare:

> In addition, the public can reduce their chances of catching the virus by following these simple but effective steps. Wash your hands regularly, and cover your mouth and nose with a tissue when you sneeze, then put the tissue in a bin – catch it, bin it, kill it.

If only the past could be ministered to as easily as swine flu, for at every turn it surfaced like a virus that proved difficult to treat.

I Beg To Move

On Monday, 24 May 2010, Mervyn Storey begged to move on marking the fortieth anniversary of the dissolution of the B-Specials and the fortieth anniversary of the Ulster Defence Regiment. He went on to commend their immense bravery in the face of the Troubles. In a speech, approximately 1,300 words long, he proceeded to eulogise the bravery of the men who defended the community 'from those who sought to murder by night'. He then proceeded to give a history of the genesis of the Ulster Special Constabulary, or B-Specials, and backed his speech up with a quote from Tim Pat Coogan who described the B-Specials as 'the rock on which the IRA foundered'. Getting a second wind he proceeded to describe the UDR in similarly glowing terms drawing attention to the fact that they were 'on active service longer than any regiment since the Napoleonic wars'. He then pointed out that the IRA had been truly trounced by these brave men:

> … it gives allegiance to, and, in many cases, is actively giving evidence to, a British police service. The republican movement has been forced to deal with decommissioning; it has been forced to announce the formal ending of its campaign; it has been forced to issue a formal stand-down order to all its personnel; and it has been forced to sign up to support the police, the courts and the rule of law.

After being challenged by Francie Molloy for misquoting, he was asked by the Speaker to bring his remarks to a close. He then delivered his last salvo:

Republican terrorists deserve no praise or commendations; they deserve no memorials. However, those whom we commemorate in the motion do deserve our thanks and appreciation.

I could not help thinking that he was channelling Lady Catherine de Bourgh from *Pride and Prejudice* who is unable to bully Elizabeth Bennet into renouncing a marriage proposal from Mr Darcy:

> I take no leave of you, Miss Bennet. I send no compliments to your mother. You deserve no such attention. I am most seriously displeased.

When Francie Molloy responded he undermined Mervyn Storey's glowing commendation of the two security forces. He spoke of the contemptible behaviour of the B-Specials towards the nationalist community. He then commented that 'this time, the croppies would not lie down'. 'Croppies Lie Down' was a famous Loyalist anti-rebel folk song which was written to express antipathy towards the 1798 United Irishmen rebels who mounted a campaign against British rule in Ireland. Ironically, their leaders were Presbyterian and they were pressing for Catholic emancipation.

> We soldiers of Erin, so proud of the name
> We'll raise on the rebels and Frenchmen our fame;
> We'll fight to the last in the honest old cause,
> And guard our religion, our freedom and laws;
> We'll fight for our country, our King and his crown,
> And make all the traitors and croppies lie down.
> Down, down, croppies lie down.

Francie Molloy pointed out that:

The B-men also opened fire on unarmed marches in Dungannon, Coalisland and across the North. The Protestant militia were at their dirty work, but this time, the croppies would not lie down; they continued to challenge. We then had the whitewash of Scarman, when it was found that the B-men were always carrying someone else's gun, no one was accountable for anything, and no one admitted playing a part.

So that is it in a nutshell: one side of the community wanted to honour and commemorate the UDR and B-Specials while the other side wanted the opposite.

May to Must is Better for Us
On 22 June 2010, Jim Wells raised the issue of flora and fauna conservation:

> Northern Ireland has lost so much, and it is now important that we turn that tide of destruction and start to rebuild our countryside. We have lost important species … I remember walking to school through fields in north Armagh where six or seven pairs of corncrakes were calling. We only have one nesting pair of chough left in Northern Ireland. Species such as lapwing and ground-wading birds such as redshank and snipe have disappeared from much of our countryside.

The Assembly was able to agree on biodiversity, and all the parties were unanimous with regard to the protection of the white-tailed eagle, the osprey, the peregrine, the barn owl and the red kite, the protection of the basking shark 'from intentional and reckless disturbance' and the hope to extend the same protection to seals, as well as the protection of the Irish hare; Edwin Poots gave an update on the Irish hare preservation strategy. He was pleased to announce that the Irish hare population was stable, and a recent survey showed that there had been 'no regression of the population's genetic strength'. In addition, he spoke about the 'all-year-round protection for the nests of certain birds that habitually use the same nest year after year, as their loss could seriously affect the breeding success of such birds'.

One of the MLAs had a reservation about blaming the loss of native species on the loss of hedgerows. He acknowledged the disappearance of the curlew and the corncrake from Fermanagh but he commented that 'elements outside of this country may be responsible for that, rather than any practices that have been undertaken here'. He went on to say 'there is one area in Crom Estate in which protected flora species have disappeared, despite the area having been fenced off and not farmed. It is all down to research and follow-up, but I agree with much of what has been said.'

It is amazing how this issue was debated without acrimony, which just goes to show that it is easier for our politicians to agree legislation on biodiversity than come to terms with the past and sorting out how to commemorate it. The Minister of the Environment commented that 'Most Members seem to be in almost complete agreement with the proposals on biodiversity; therefore, I do not intend to prolong this part of the debate.'

The Agreement copper-fastened power-sharing as a key principle. Safeguards were put in place to ensure that both communities would have a fair say. In theory it was a landmark agreement which created a power-sharing executive using the D'Hondt system. It ensured that ministerial portfolios would be shared between main parties and mandatory cross-community voting was to be used for major decisions.

The Assembly was even able to use more definite language in their legislation: the Good Friday Agreement's 'may' in relation to North–South ministerial appointments was replaced with the stronger 'must'. 'May' expresses possibility whereas 'must' expresses a stronger obligation. To strengthen biodiversity legislation the Minister of the Environment amended the legislation to read 'The Department must …'. Danny Kinahan, UUP, praised the change: 'I welcome amendment No 1, which proposes to change the word "may" to "must".' He also said that:

> This is where the Assembly is at its best – making Northern Ireland a better place to live for us and for the wildlife.

During this speech he questioned whether people in the councils understood the meaning of the word 'biodiversity' and commented that there was no such word in the Oxford Dictionary. He said, 'We have to find a plain English way to communicate this down to those on the ground.'

On 30 June 2010, Edwin Poots spoke on the Clean Neighbourhoods and Environment Bill: Second Stage. The bill was being introduced to deal with 'low-level' environmental crime:

> Littering
> Dog fouling
> Graffiti
> Fly-posting
> Fly-tipping
> Irresponsible parking
> Abandoned vehicles
> Abandoned shopping trolleys
> Unwanted behaviour in back alleys
> Nuisance that is caused by noise
> Audible intruder alarms
> False alarms
> Light pollution

Plastic bags
Paper bags
Broken glass
Empty bottles
Used nappies
Crisp packets
Chewing gum
Cigarette butts
Alley-gaters
Eyesores
Drug dealing
Domestic burglary
Alcohol abuse
Underage drinking
General bad manners
Barking dogs
Stray dogs

Proposed measures to deal with low-level environmental crime included:

Fixed penalties
ASBOs
Alley gating
Banning dogs from restricted areas
Requiring dogs to be kept on a lead
Restricting the number of dogs that can be walked by one person

On the whole I felt that the Assembly dealt with the Clean Neighbourhoods and Environment Bill in an exemplary manner. Even a little humour was used in an exchange between Alastair Ross and Maurice Morrow:

During my time at university, it was common practice for many students to wheel shopping trolleys into the halls of residence or leave them outside the door. It is important that—
Lord Morrow: That is students for you.
Mr Ross: Absolutely. Now that I am not a student, I can speak from the moral high ground.

On 30 June 2010, Dominic Bradley raised a topic which was painful to listen to. It concerned the Reavey family murders in 1976. No human being could read about these horrific murders without feeling a sense of revulsion. Dominic Bradley went on to catalogue the murders of three members of the Reavey family. Although Mr Reavey, the father of the murdered men, pleaded for no retaliation, these indiscriminate murders of young Catholic men led to an equally horrendous tit-for-tat strike, the Kingsmill massacre, where ten Protestant mill workers were gunned down on their way home from work. Members of the Reavey family were present during the discussion of this topic. What suffering they must have endured and continue to endure? What suffering the relatives of the Kingsmill massacre endured and continue to endure? The debate was in danger of descending into a tit-for-tat of what Danny Kennedy called 'a tribal jamboree of blame, counterblame and "whataboutery"'. There was a sense, as he pointed out, that these shocking slaughters struck fear into the community. He said, 'Lives were taken, lives were broken, and lives were changed forever.'

> Other massacres were mentioned
> The words ricocheted round
> The house like the bullets
> That sprayed the victims
> Nobody wanted to take the blame
> Everyone wanted to blame the other side

Everyone wanted to set it in context
One man's context is another man's banjax
One man's collusion is another man's cooperation
One man's meat is another man's poison
One man's guilt is another man's absolution.
One man's killer is another man's deliverer
One man's terrorist is another man's freedom fighter
One man's testimony is another man's whitewash
One man's fabrication is another man's proof
One man's calumny is another man's panegyric
One man's smear is another man's cheer
One man's applause is another man's jeer
One man's jest is another man's jibe
One man's condemnation is another man's commendation
One man's success is another man's fiasco
One man's denunciation is another man's recommendation
One man's blessing is another man's curse
One man's jinx is another man's mascot
One man's belief is another man's scepticism
One man's religion is another man's apostasy
One man's tradition is another man's oppression
One man's road is another man's cul-de-sac
One man's drum is another man's truncheon
One man's salamander is another man's gerrymander
One man's song is another man's jeremiad
One man's eulogy is another man's tirade
One man's homily is another man's polemic
One man's speech is another man's rant
One man's oration is another man's tongue-lashing
One man's talk is another man's invective
One man's serenade is another man's charivari
One man's informant is another man's tout
One man's route is another man's sacred space

One man's goal is another man's target
One man's biting point is another man's breaking point
Ones man's opinion is another man's bigotry
One man's philippic is another man's brainwashing
One man's integrity is another man's perfidy
One man's honour is another man's dishonesty
One man's amnesty is another man's travesty
One man's storm is another man's storm in a teacup
One man's charm is another man's jinx
One man's *mise-en-scène* is another man's *mise en abyme*
One man's *Magic Flute* is another man's *Dido and Aeneas*
One man's Armani is another man's Matalan
One man's Rolex is another man's Timex
One man's flower is another man's weed
One man's prince is another man's toad
One man's peace is another man's war
One man's home rule is another man's Rome rule
One man's land is another man's plantation
One man's tenure is another man's usurpation
One man's gathering is another man's unlawful assembly
One man's solution is another man's compromise

I wonder how many politicians have to raise such matters from the murderous past? The Troubles was like an unquiet ghost watching from the public gallery looking for answers to questions – like Puck, the ghost of Malahide, who haunts the castle from generation to generation. Is it true that unquiet ghosts can never be put to rest? Can deeds be so heinous that they cannot be forgotten but continue to surface? Is this part of the post-conflict journey? How can we put the past to rest? How can victims get closure? After apartheid in South Africa the Truth and Reconciliation Commission was established to deal with the legacy of the past. Those people who had suffered violations were invited to give statements; perpetrators were also encouraged to give testimonials regarding the part they had played in the conflict. Should Northern Ireland have a Truth and Reconciliation Commission? Some process is surely needed to deal with all the unanswered questions, unsolved murders and unexplained disappearances.

There were three strands to the Agreement and three strands to dealing with the post-conflict era, as suggested by Hugh Orde. He made this comment in 2004, some six years after the Good Friday Agreement:

> In previous reflections on this subject I have advanced the view that there are three broad strands to dealing with history, namely, conciliation, compensation, and investigation. These three strands must also be supported by a legal underpinning of the entire process.

One minute the Assembly is discussing the introduction of a plastic bag tax or the fate of the golden plover, and the next minute the issues from the past emerge like children who come out of nowhere when the ice cream van plays its merry jingle.

On 13 December 2010, Ms Lo, Alliance Party, raised the question of the Assembly's offices in Shanghai and Hong Kong. It was good that the Assembly were discussing foreign markets and considering trade missions to the Far East.

On 23 March 2011, Mr Speaker asked ministers to lay aside their disagreements in order to celebrate the successes of the devolved Assembly commenting that this was the first Assembly to finish a full term in a generation:

> We have held 277 plenary sittings and approved some 69 Bills.
> Ministers have taken over 11,624 questions for oral answer and
> 32,411 questions for written answer. That, in itself, is historic.

The Speaker then thanked everyone who worked in the building – not only the politicians but the staff who look after the building. First Minister Peter Robinson continued in the complimentary tone set by the Speaker and congratulated the folk on the hill:

> We secured a record £2.6 billion of inward commitments for investment and
> £500 million in annual salaries … We extended free travel to everyone
> over 60 years of age, and there are now 61,000 SmartPasses in circulation.
> Some five and a half million journeys have been made …
> We have purchased more than 200 new buses and 20 new trains.
> That is another record. By the end of the term,
> we will have passed almost 70 Bills in the Assembly.
> The Executive have reached more than 1,600 proposals by agreement.

The deputy first minister, Martin McGuinness, echoed the words of the first minister and even spoke of the Blair days, the despair days, the Chuckle Brothers (himself and Paisley) and the current configuration of himself and Peter Robinson (the Brothers Grimm). He even found time to thank the cleaners – in fact, he went into some detail about how he had built up a good relationship with the women who cleaned the building:

> Most importantly, I thank the women from all parts of Belfast who clean the Building when we are not here. I always make a point of speaking to them, and I have great friendships with many of them. On my way in this morning, I met a woman who is 77 years of age. She has been here for 11 years; she has been with us during all that time.

Martin McGuinness spoke of his arrival at Stormont after the English ministers had left and even mentioned that the English ministers had taken the light bulbs with them! He congratulated Ian Paisley, who was the first minister of the new Assembly before Peter Robinson assumed the position, and thanked his wife, Eileen Paisley:

> I thank him and his good wife, Eileen, both of whom I regard as huge friends of the peace process and friends of mine.

When Mr Elliott took the floor he also acknowledged the cleaning ladies, but wanted the male cleaning staff to be acknowledged also:

> I noted that the deputy First Minister thanked the cleaning ladies, but I want to include the gentlemen cleaners because there are a number of them here as well. I am afraid that he was being sexist in that respect, but we will call it quits at that.

What I found strange about this session, about the Assembly setting aside their disagreements to celebrate their successes, was the failure to mention the elephant in the room. I felt that the ministers were avoiding the real issue by complimenting the ancillary staff and referring to their friendships. Because the Assembly had survived a full term, the first in a generation, they decided that their relationships weren't so bad after all. Patsy McGlone alluded to the contentious character of the Assembly but he acknowledged that 'members have got to know one another and maybe established friendships'. He said, 'I hope that we will ultimately lay the building blocks for the trust that is so necessary to bring about reconciliation in this part of our country, the reconciliation for which the people of Ireland have yearned for so many years.'

The Speaker even invited Dr Paisley (now Lord Bannside), whom he referred to as the 'Father of the House', to say a few words. My concern here is that although the MLAs were so chuffed to have pulled off a term of office, their friendships were superficial.

Mr Elliott pointed out that the rate of unemployment was extremely high – he injected some reality into the backslapping session. He also pointed out that, 'Although we can look at our successes in the Assembly, we cannot forget the failure of the Executive to meet for over five months.'

My feeling here was that the fathers and sons of the House were speaking at the end of this four-year stint of government, but where were the mothers and daughters? There was something essentially patriarchal about the clever men congratulating themselves on their new Bills and buses and their billions of inward investment and then complimenting the cleaning ladies, thereby reinforcing gender roles.

After Easter, a play by Anne Devlin, highlighted the fragility of the period prior to the peace process. It was first performed in Stratford 1994, a year punctuated by milestones leading up to the Good Friday Agreement: the IRA ceased military action; the British and Irish governments and the IRA made reciprocal concessions; the broadcasting ban which precluded Sinn Féin from the Irish airwaves was scrapped; and the embargo preventing Sinn Féin President Gerry Adams entering the U.S. was removed. Exploratory talks between Sinn Féin and the British government had been promised, yet the frailty and volatility of such tentative moves towards peace were exemplified when, in the same year, six Catholic men died in a horrific gun attack as they watched a World Cup match in a pub in Loughinisland, Co. Down. Sara Ruddick wrote:

> War surrounds us. Everywhere, it seems, men and sometimes women are fighting...Those who live in the absence of declared war—in what passes for peace—witness the tribal nationalism, racialism, domination, and imperialism that remind us why peace so often seems only a temporary cessation of hostilities.

Northern Ireland remained an unstable society even while the way towards peace was being paved in 1994. Women were central to this burgeoning post-war peace process. Social scientist Noeleen Heyzer states:

> Women have a crucial role to play in the rebuilding of stable societies. International and regional initiatives to link peace with justice not only benefit women, but are also strengthened by them. During the transition to peace, a unique opportunity exists to put in place a gender-responsive framework for a country's reconstruction based on the three dimensions of justice: legal justice to address discriminatory laws against women at institutional and policy levels, such as inheritance laws that prevent women from owning property; restorative justice to address violation of human rights and war crimes so that people can move beyond their trauma and begin to construct new lives for themselves; and distributive justice to address structural and systematic injustices such as the political, economic and social inequalities that are frequently the underlying causes of conflict.

In fact, the Northern Ireland peace process could not have been brokered and sustained without the help of women and the influence they brought to these three dimensions of justice. Sociologist Rosemary Sales outlines their contribution:

The early 1990s witnessed a tremendous upsurge of energy and creativity by women in Northern Ireland. The range of groups and organisations established included enormous numbers of women, many of whom became involved for the first time with 'women's issues'. The ceasefires provided an impetus for this movement, opening up the possibilities of fundamental change in Northern Ireland.

Added to that, the elephant in the room was getting bigger and bigger with every speech. I could see that congratulating the cleaning ladies on their hard work was a red herring, an avoidance tactic. Basically the Assembly's D'Hondt system of proportional representation ensured that rivals ended up closer to each other. Therefore there's an argument to suggest that the D'Hondt system should be dumped as it stymies real cooperation.

I have tried to spot patterns in the Hansard reports I have studied, and I think that the members of the Assembly seem to swing between the two extremes of cooperation and obstruction. The past lingers like an unexploded mine, the kind that are left buried in the ground after a war and can be uncovered when the land is dug up or disturbed. The past is like a wrecking ball that threatens to destroy the fragile infrastructure.

Leave no Stone Unturned

'Come' they told him
Pa rum pum pum pum
A new consensus to form
Pa rum pum pum pum
The issues were marches
Pa rum pum pum pum
And flags and drums
Pa rum pum pum pum,

Dr Brenda Josephine Liddy

And of course the past
Rum pum pum pum
Leave no stone unturned
Rum pum pum pum.

Making Sense of Lewis Carroll's Nonsense Fantasies

> 'It was much pleasanter at home,' thought poor Alice, 'when one wasn't always growing larger and smaller, and being ordered about by mice and rabbits. I almost wish I hadn't gone down that rabbit-hole—and yet—and yet —it's rather curious, you know, this sort of life! I do wonder what *can* have happened to me! When I used to read fairy-tales, I fancied that kind of thing never happened, and now here I am in the middle of one! There ought to be a book written about me, that there ought! And when I grow up, I'll write one —but I'm grown up now,' she added in a sorrowful tone; 'at least there's no room to grow up any more *here*.'

Each new school term presented a range of terrors for me, but summer term was probably the worst because of the lawnmower. John, the groundsman-cum-caretaker, used to take delight in pounding up and down the grounds with that infernal machine. Not only did I hate the sound, but the smell of freshly cut grass made me sick. Christmas was also grim. I hated the Christmas tree in the reception and the tinsel that suddenly appeared out of the store. I especially hated red tinsel – what was wrong with people suddenly wanting a sea of tinsel, lights and baubles? The teachers adapted their resources to get the most out of the event: the English teacher who was normally a reasonably organised person with a logical lesson plan deviated into a silly role play. After reading a pointless story written by Charles Dickens about a Christmas miser who finally got a conscience after a series of ghostly visitations, she divided the class into three groups. Of course when the word group was mentioned I had one of my meltdowns, but it was okay because I was allowed to observe. The object of the lesson was to understand the values that prevailed in Victorian society, so one group had to research Charles Dickens' life, the other Victorian London and the third group Charles's characterisations.

I didn't understand anything as abstract as ghosts, so my teaching assistant explained that ghosts were just his fears about growing old and that ghosts didn't exist. I asked, 'Why did Dickens just not call the ghosts Ebenezer Scrooge's fears?'

'Because,' my teaching assistant replied, 'Dickens was a fiction writer and therefore he made up stories.'

'So he was lying,' I said.

'It's called fiction,' she replied.

She wrote out a new version of the story in which Scrooge was growing old and he began to fear death. The stinginess which had defined his character was no longer an incentive. As he walked through the city streets he saw even the poorest families preparing for Christmas Day. For the first time in his life he saw the excitement in the children's eyes. He remembered that he was once a child, and even though his mother and father were poor they always hung a stocking at the end of his bed, and when he woke up on Christmas morning there was always an orange inside the stocking and some kind of toy. When his father died of overwork and exhaustion, his mother fell into deep despair and withdrew from him. She sent him to work as an apprentice to a merchant called Fezziwig, a jolly man who had the power to make their lives 'a pleasure or a toil'. At this stage he met the love of his life, Belle, and he was truly happy for the first time. They met at one of the lavish Christmas parties that Fezziwig threw for his employees. But his happiness was not to last because love is like a plant and if you do not water it and give it care and attention, it will die. The reason ... When Fezziwig died, Scrooge and his friend Jacob Marley started a little import–export business as well as having a warehouse and a counting house. They were quite successful, but, unfortunately, to build up a business from scratch in those days was not easy. Scrooge became so immersed in making his business a success that he neglected Belle. When she dropped into the warehouse he would have been deep in conversation with Marley about the price of rice and the cost of cotton and coffee. All he wanted to discuss with her was the tariff on tea, the tax on teak and the highs and lows of trading in an expanding empire. As his business grew, a sign went up on the warehouse, 'Marley and Scrooge', and Belle felt eclipsed by the exigencies of silk, satin and seeds. In the year 1843 the sun never set on the empire and Scrooge never went to bed. London was the epicentre of this quickly expanding empire, and Scrooge wanted to make hay when the sun was shining. He never noticed how unhappy Belle was, and when she brought up the topic of their future he just ignored her. 'You have changed so much,' she declared. 'If you are not counting money and putting price tags on your merchandise, you are counting the lumps of coal you put on the fire.' Scrooge was brazen enough to believe that Belle wouldn't find anyone better than him; in the world of the workhouse surely he was a good catch! Things came to a head one Christmas when Scrooge, a man inundated with the goods of the empire from jute to juniper, forgot to give Belle a gift. He usually gave her a jar of candied fruit which he took out of his warehouse (and one year he even forgot to take off the price tag). He knew the face value, the asking price and the market value of all his merchandise but not the worth of love as pure as Belle's. The prospect of the workhouse was his constant bogeymen and the idea that he would ever have to rely on charity was his bugbear. A few days after Christmas Belle said to Scrooge, 'Ebenezer, you have changed so much. All you care about are the prices of your spices, the cost of your cumin. I am so happy that you have made a success of your business but you have become obsessed with it.' Ebenezer, so eloquent about the nuances of nutmeg and so exacting about aniseed, so careful about cardamom and so fastidious about fenugreek, was unable to muster up a few words to curry favour with the love of his life and so let her walk out of his life and his counting room forever.

Time went on and Ebenezer Scrooge and Jacob Marley ran their business in mutual harmony. They were never going to be millionaires but they were never going to go under either. They were like two oxen yoked together and committed to trudging through a landscape of profit and loss, buying and selling, keeping an eye on the stock market and tracking its fluctuations and oscillations. Victorian times were not characterised by boom and bust cycles, and two gentlemen of the cautious calibre of Scrooge and Marley were not likely to take risks or put their business in jeopardy. They had a simple marketing strategy which entailed selling their goods for a higher amount than they had purchased them and factoring in their variable and fixed charges. All their conversations revolved around markups and margins and break-even points. They never used the word discount or commission and they had no middlemen to pay.

As time went on Marley was getting frailer and less enamoured with conversations about profit and loss, and he had the temerity to suggest hiring a clerk. At this stage in his life Scrooge, disentangled from any romantic attachments and unfettered with the feared prospect of starting a family and having little mouths to feed, felt completely fulfilled and had no wish to hire and pay a clerk. Not only that, but he would have had to provide an office for him, a chair and a desk, and there was every likelihood that he would be a miserable creature dredged up from some pitiful slum whose only aim in life would be to get heat and food. He imagined that this wretched soul would eventually try to outfox him and start pilfering from him – small larcenies at first and then bigger heists. Ebenezer thought that there was no better business partner in the world than Marley and no higher form of human interaction on earth than two savvy men discussing the vagaries of the spice market, their outgoings and expenses, their plans to expand, their schemes to make a killing and their strategies to earn another sixpence. Scrooge never wanted any high days or holidays as making money was better than any holiday he had ever had. Anyone seeing the two men conversing together in the cold counting house in the dark days of winter with their long coats and gloves on would have pitied them but at the same time envied their seeming oblivion to everything not associated with trade. But there was another world out there, outside of commerce! Not everything revolved around trade, export and import, buying and selling, merchandise and stock. There was a bustling, rushing, hustling world just outside their door and that world was preparing for Christmas. Farmers were bringing geese and turkeys to market; poulterers were pulling their necks and hanging them in their shops. Women were baking Christmas puddings and men were making toys for their children. Another big festival in the year is Easter, but, again, this did not impinge on the two men as their year was not punctuated by the liturgical calendar but rather with the ebb and flow of cargo deliveries from the subcontinent.

Scrooge tortured himself with these musings for many weeks and was on the point of pulling rank and pointing out the folly of hiring this potential employee who would wreak havoc, pull the wool over their eyes and become a liability. However, although the hiring of a clerk did not fit with their overall financial strategy, Marley's death accelerated the need for assistance, and, in the end, one Bob Cratchit was hired.

To say that Scrooge mourned the loss of Marley would have meant attributing an emotional literacy to him which, of course, he didn't have. To say that the death of his business partner did not affect him whatsoever would have been to accuse him of having no heart or empathy whatsoever. For one thing, he never changed the sign over the business, and he admitted to one of his traders that he missed the cut and thrust of their conversations. Over the years Marley and he had built up a network of wheelers and dealers, merchants and agents, and they felt proud of their confederacy of connections. However, Scrooge had to acknowledge that it was Marley who kept the business thriving – he was good at keeping everyone happy, and, in a way, he was Scrooge's human face. With him gone, Scrooge wasn't able to step into his shoes, and this had a knock-on effect on his business. His other business associates complained about his brusque manner and his patent meanness.

His treatment of his clerk, Bob Cratchit, was legendary. Instead of teaching him the business and showing him the ropes, Scrooge treated him like a necessary evil and made his working life an endless drudge. He didn't want Bob to get his feet under the table or to steal a march on him, so he kept his distance and rebutted his sole employee's opening gambits of conversation. Working for Scrooge was not the best career move for anyone, but, at the same time, in a world where there was no welfare state, any job was better than none. In the late spring and summer months the counting house was reasonably warm, but in the winter it was unbearably cold. Poor Bob Cratchit used to appear at work dressed in a large overcoat with a long woollen scarf and knitted hat and never once dared cast off his outer clothing. His wife was of the opinion that her husband's employer brought penny-pinching to a new level and wondered what sort of a man would intentionally cause his employee to have chilblains.

As time went on Bob Cratchit accepted that he would never be on friendly terms with Scrooge and that his office would never be redecorated nor would he ever have a warm fire. He knew that the lumps of coal would be rationed out as if there was some kind of war on and austerity was the order of the day. But he was a decent man and tried to see the good in his employer. He would say to his wife, 'It must be terrible to go home to an empty house and have no one to talk over the day's affairs with or to share a meal or an anecdote with.' His wife would reply, 'He had Belle and he treated her badly. She had a lucky escape.'

Inadvertently Scrooge's stinginess helped other people to feel more magnanimous. He became a yardstick for parsimony and his name became part of the lexicon. Rabelais' fictional character Gargantua was the origin for the adjective 'gargantuan'. Charles Perrault's Bluebeard became synonymous with a murderous husband. Mentor was Odysseus's adviser in Homer's Odyssey and the word came to mean guide or counsellor. Scrooge was insensible to these unintended consequences and each year he become more wizened and withdrawn. As the Tao says:

> Difficult and easy bring about each other
> Long and short reveal each other
> High and low support each other
> Music and voice harmonize each other.

Even a broken clock is right two times a day.

So what made Scrooge change into a man who would send Bob Cratchit out to buy another coal scuttle and anonymously provide a prize turkey for a Christmas dinner, who would suddenly make generous donations to good causes and dote on Tiny Tim, Cratchit's ill child?

The fact was that the ghost who visited Scrooge was no more than the pangs of conscience that creep up on every man when he reaches a certain age, when not only have his parents died but he loses members of his own generation. As a mother's pangs in labour lead to the birth of a baby, Scrooge's twinges of conscience gave rise to his change of heart. He tried to block out the shock he felt when Marley, his business partner, died. Although he wouldn't have regarded him as his bosom buddy – he didn't cultivate relationships, he missed their daily chats about the way they had cozened the poor, the buyers and the brokers. They would never tire of discussing the London Stock Exchange, the stocks and shares, financial markets and railway stock, and they would have liked to pass themselves off as reputable traders when they swanned off in their most respectable clothes to carry out their transactions. Their appearance and general countenance looked slightly staged as their suits were short of being shabby and they didn't bother to engage with any of the other traders. Marley's clothes were slightly ill-fitting and his arms were too long for his jacket. He always walked behind Scrooge like a harlequin out of a play. Scrooge's apparel belonged to a bygone era, and his coat hung on him as if he was a scarecrow. On closer inspection you would have seen little stains of snuff on his off-white shirt, and there was a button missing from his waistcoat. Other members of the exchange would had tipped their hats to them but wouldn't engage any further with these two bachelors who had gone beyond a women's touch to enter a land of sartorial dilapidation.

For the truth was that they only attended the exchange to give some respectability to their moneylending business. That was why they had a series of cashboxes kept well out of sight, padlocked up multiple times and secured in the basement each evening. Sadly the two men were nothing better than usurers and their extortionate moneylending practices led to much misery. Scrooge lived in an era of the dreaded workhouse and people would have tried any means to avoid being carted off to them, but each time they borrowed money from Scrooge and Marley it brought them closer to this infamous institution where food was scarce and charity rare. In literature dating back to ancient times usurers have been vilified. Plato and Plutarch condemned it, and in the Old Testament Ezekiel remonstrated, 'If he has exacted usury or taken increase – shall he live? He shall not live! If he has done any of these abominations, he shall surely die; his blood shall be upon him.' In the Middle Ages, Dante, an Italian poet, reserved a place for usurers in 'the inner ring of the seventh circle of hell'. And, of course, Marx denounced usury in the twentieth century. So, in effect, these two gentlemen created suffering for their debtors when they defaulted on their payments. Scrooge even approved of the workhouse because in his estimation if you were not capable of staying financially solvent, you were better off in it. He had heard stories about the horrendous conditions, the overcrowding, the dreadful food and how families were separated from each other, but he was not too bothered about them. In his opinion a debt is a debt which must be repaid. Look at the hours he put into achieving his wealth! Meagre meals and mean accommodation, no holidays, no luxuries and no skiving or shirking of duty were the order of the day.

When you think of it, the ghosts could be taken out of *A Christmas Carol* and you would still have the story because the story is about the hero having a change of heart. If you plotted against the framework of Joseph Campbell's *The Hero's Journey*, you would find that Scrooge was making his courageous journey. The first stage is the ordinary world where Scrooge beavered from morning to night in the Cornhill area near the London Stock Exchange and The East India Trading Company. Then, in the second stage, he experiences his call to adventure after the death of his partner, Marley. In the third stage Scrooge dismissed the call of his conscience by passing off his pangs of guilt as a bout of indigestion. In the fourth stage his nephew Fred probably stands for his mentor as Fred still has a zest for life. In the fifth stage Scrooge resolves to pay Fred a visit and wish him a merry Christmas, but he hasn't the ability to reach out. In the sixth stage he feels a strong desire to go back to the *bah humbug* mentality, and before he reaches the seventh stage of the approach he nearly reverts to type. However, he has some nobility in his soul, and although it is an ordeal for him to create a new identity and enter the special world, he does. Joseph Campbell argues that the hero journeys from the ordinary, mundane world in order to enter the special heroic world where he will be tested and tried until he has obtained his goal. He moves on from seven to eight, and then he gains his reward in the ninth stage. His reward is to share his riches with the poor and unfortunate in his family and in his firm. The mean, old Scrooge dies and a new Scrooge emerges and makes many generous gestures instead of fleecing his debtors. In phase ten he takes the road back after he has connected with his humanity. He opens his coffers and caskets, once sealed with locks and chains like his heart, and enters into the true spirit of Christmas. Elements from his past may re-emerge to haunt him; he may cast a longing glance towards the London Stock Exchange and will himself to be there in the midst of the bloodthirsty wheeling and dealing of the traders and brokers. How he loved to get one up on the market, to pull a fast one, to spot a trend or predict a slump. Now he was spending his time doing acts of mercy and divesting himself of the hard-earned cash that he had stashed away for years. He found that giving was more exhausting than amassing; skimping and scrimping suited him. He was goal-orientated and his goal was gold. You knew where you stood with saving and stashing, and his journey from miser to philanthropist was not always easy. Humouring Tiny Tim, Bob Cratchit's invalid son, proved to be very taxing. Maybe it was because Tim with his boundless goodness and his frailty was such a contrast to Scrooge's covetous nature and his wiry physique. Tiny Tim was always counting his meagre blessings, and a benediction seemed to flow from his very presence. A cripple boy on a crutch who lived in abject poverty was richer in spirit than the wizened and heart-shrivelled Scrooge who was always counting his money. A hero's journey is not always a smooth one, and our hero still has to go through stages eleven and twelve where he is severely tested.

In *The Writers' Journey* Christopher Vogler writes, 'At the climax the hero is severely tested once more on the threshold of home. He or she is purified by a last sacrifice, another moment of death and rebirth, but on a higher and more complete level.'

Transforming from a miser to a philanthropist is beset with trials and tribulations. Sometimes Scrooge suffered a pang of regret at not spending his every waking hour amassing a fortune; spending time with his nephew and the Cratchit family sometimes seemed like a waste of time – you didn't get paid for being kind to your relatives. Sometimes he felt he had taken leave of his senses such was the powerful pull of materialism, but he had grown so fond of Tiny Tim who had now become his pet project. If he could rescue Tiny Tim, he would be redeemed – he could wipe out his covetous sins. Sometimes he wanted to take Tiny Tim into his counting house and show him how money was made, how he had slaved over his accounts from morning to night, how he had perused the stocks and shares and how he had pursued his debtors. He had always seen Christmas as a pickpocket robbing him of his hard-working clerk for a whole day. He used to wonder why anyone wanted to lose a day's pay and then go out and squander money on geese and gifts. It did not make good business sense to deliberately divest yourself of your hard-earned money.

In stage twelve the hero returns with the elixir. As Vogler comments, 'The hero returns home or continues the journey, bearing some element of the treasure that has the power to transform the world as the hero has been transformed'. Or, as the maestro Charles Dickens himself writes:

> Scrooge was better than his word. He did it all, and infinitely more; and to Tiny Tim, who did not die, he was a second father. He became as good a friend, as good a master, and as good a man, as the good old city knew, or any other good old city, town, or borough, in the good old world. Some people laughed to see the alteration in him, but he let them laugh, and little heeded them; for he was wise enough to know that nothing ever happened on this globe, for good, at which some people did not have their fill of laughter in the outset; and knowing that such as these would be blind anyway, he thought it quite as well that they should wrinkle

up their eyes in grins, as have the malady in less attractive forms. His own heart laughed: and that was quite enough for him.

And, of course, his journey from miser to magnanimous soul, from penny-pincher to philanthropist, from Scrooge to Santa Claus was so profound that:

> He had no further intercourse with Spirits, but lived upon the Total Abstinence Principle, ever afterwards; and it was always said of him, that he knew how to keep Christmas well, if any man alive possessed the knowledge. May that be truly said of us, and all of us! And so, as Tiny Tim observed, God bless Us, Every One!

Good Friday's Child and the Good Friday Agreement

An American jetting into Ireland with a dossier on the North's post-conflict disputes was nothing new. Bill Clinton had been active in the 1998 Good Friday Agreement, and he had flown over the same stormy Atlantic with the same hopes and fears as Richard Haass. Descending over Belfast Lough on the approach to Belfast International, Richard couldn't help admiring the patchwork of fields that was becoming visible. Green was the dominant colour, but, of course, he would soon be encountering orange – the other dominant hue in the political palette. He thought of his book, *Foreign Policy Begins at Home: The Case for Putting America's House in Order*, and how he had speculated on America's need to fix her economy before stamping into other countries to sort out their problems – although his present business in coming to deal with Northern Ireland's unresolved issues sort of undermined his philosophy. Alas, he reflected, the world is like a mirror where we can see everyone's faults except our own. As the plane landed he put George Mitchell's *Making Peace* into his hand baggage. He noted that the subtitle read: 'The behind-the-scenes story of the negotiations that culminated in the signing of the Northern Ireland Peace Accord. Told by the American Senator who served as independent chairman of the talks'. On another edition he had noticed the subheading: 'The inside story of the making of the Good Friday Agreement'. The subheadings of the different editions suggested a kind of conspiratorial world of cloak-and-dagger scenarios, hidden agendas, back channels, draft documents and multi-party talks. The brinkmanship was more terrifying than a bullfight. One minute the Agreement was the only show in town and the next it was the worst treachery on the face of the earth. Indeed poor George had many hoops to jump through before getting a yes. Haass suddenly wished he had a Father Alec Reid to bless him, to act as an angelic arbitrator; a Mo Mowlam to run round the executive parties like a magic bullet, urging assent; a General John de Chastelain to decommission the guns; a Tony Blair to pull strings from Westminster; a Bertie Ahern to work behind the scenes on cross-border agencies; an Ian Paisley for a last-minute conversion; a Gerry Adams for his diplomacy; and even a Nelson Mandela to cheer from the sidelines. He wondered if he could handle the clandestine backstage all-party talks and inter-party negotiations with agendas slipping away like the changing mists over the Cavehill. He recalled the words of a song he had heard by Colum Sands, 'Whatever you Say, Say Nothing'.

He could imagine his wife back in New York rolling her eyes and commenting, 'Richard, for heaven's sake, do you need to cart all those books onto the plane?' She was one of those top executives who could manage her whole life on her BlackBerry while he needed a library of books, a plethora of electronic gadgets and a constant stream of news.

Before he touched down on the runway he knew that his arrival wouldn't be like the opening scene from *Love Actually* with a Hugh Grant voiceover:

> It seems to me that love is everywhere. Often, it's not particularly dignified or newsworthy, but it's always there – fathers and sons, mothers and daughters, husbands and wives, boyfriends, girlfriends, old friends.

Northern Ireland's agreements reminded him of Tibetan tulpas – 'magical emanations, conjured things or phantoms'. These conjured beings usually started out as friendly Friar Tuck but had a tendency to get out of control and needed to be destroyed.

He saw some of the people in the North as victims of witnessing too much aggression; he saw them as the sons and daughters that Bandura wrote about in his social learning theory – that their aggression was a learnt behaviour. Bandura conducted an experiment where children were shown a video of a subject pummelling and beating a Bobo doll. The group of children exposed to this behaviour then mimicked it. The Good Friday Agreement was like a beautiful Bobo doll, and the naysayers and critics had verbally assaulted it and tried to destroy it.

The Past, The Flags, The Parades Have Not Gone Away

    Come, they said, we need
        The Agreement to succeed
    Haas was an American envoy
    Have you magic powers to bring
    They asked Hass
    Can you change the past?
    Have you magic powers to bring
        He tried his level best
    He was put to the test

Richard spent the first few weeks meeting the heads and representatives of the five executive parties. Talking to them he was reminded of a story he once heard about a woman who goes into confession. After telling the priest of her husband's numerous faults, the priest said, 'I do not want to hear your husband's confession, I want to hear yours.' He thought that if there was a Nobel Prize for enumerating other parties' faults, these politicians would be winners. He always felt that there was a clear distinction between a war of necessity and a war of choice, and Northern Ireland had been handed this pristine agreement wrought in the pain and agony of thirty years of trauma, fashioned by the greatest leaders and diplomats in the Western world, guns had been melted into ploughshares and still it was not enough.

    He felt an urge to say to the parties who were making the submission, 'Why don't you value what you've got? Why don't you treasure each other and make this work?' But he knew this kind of discourse was more suited to a marriage counselling session and not a diplomatic meeting. Still, as the weeks went past and he spoke to hundreds of political representatives and garnered hundreds of submissions, he had the sinking feeling that he was not getting anywhere. Although the guns had gone, the terrorists had gone, the ex-prisoners were walking the streets and the two main rival parties, the DUP and Sinn Féin, were sitting together in a power-sharing Assembly, the past had not gone away. The past was like a minefield, and every time a leader tried to bring forward an initiative a mine was triggered. L.P. Hartley's *The Go-Between* opened with the lines, 'The past is a foreign country: they do things differently there', and he related to this quote on two levels: instead of being a diplomat he felt like a doormat scurrying between the two main factions and receiving submissions which were not about moving forward but about staying put forever. Secondly, the way they dealt with the past was different: they refused to draw a line in the sand, instead they dug their trenches deeper, and there was a distinct hint of 'No Surrender'. Lines in the sand became scores on the blame card. He got the impression that the parties were only interested in their own demands rather than looking at the bigger picture. He tried to find common ground, but it was difficult when he remained, in effect, an intermediary and the lack of plenary discussions stymied the negotiations. He felt that the politicians were living in a time warp and were denying themselves and their communities fresh ideas and new policies which would break the spell of the past that seemed to enthral them. He understood the challenges of letting go of the past and believed that victims' legacies should be acknowledged but not at the cost of arresting future progress.

Sometimes when he was listening to the submissions he was reminded of a radio broadcast: each party blasted out its own particular ideology and then switched off; there didn't seem to be the will for one party to listen to another party's broadcast. The ironic thing was that the politicians had such great integrity and they wanted the best for their communities, but the past was like a restless ghost which hung over the power-sharing executive like Banquo's ghost in *Macbeth*. 'Blood will have blood' and revenge will have revenge.

There is only so much a mediator can do and as Christmas tightened its grip Richard had a sense of disappointment. He understood that the protagonists had to meet behind closed doors during the lead-up to the Good Friday Agreement, but surely the democratic process was more robust than that after thirteen years?

He felt that the country was plagued by its conscience. The people were deeply religious, but this religion was allied to a profound sense of identity which had become a stumbling block to peace. They needed a confessor not a diplomat.

I Cannot Believe it's Not the Parades Commission

'Go', they told him
You did not succeed
    This was the word on the street,
He ran out of time
He had no magic powers to bring,
He was manipulative
He had nothing to tell us
He did his best for us
    But we honour him

At the pivotal point, with the able assistance of his vice-chair, Meghan O'Sullivan, Richard worked round the clock and the draft was delivered. Sometimes he had moments of euphoria and he could see the past melting into a sea of oblivion – melting like the guns and weapons which were decommissioned in 1998. He saw the disputes over the contentious parades being resolved. He had a vision that the Union Jack and the Irish tricolour could coexist like the lion and the lamb in the Book of Isaiah, chapter 11; the two flags could be flown together, or a new flag could be designed. It was not beyond the realm of possibility to have a new flag which would reflect the identity of each community.

However, after an all-night session behind closed doors, behind the scenes, on 22 December, he saw his vision evaporate like a mirage in the desert. The only promised land for Haass was the departure lounge in Dublin Airport and an assortment of comments which included:

He was in cahoots with others.
What more compromise can there be?
There are now terrorists in government.
The RUC is gone.

The talks must stall.
Haass must go home.
He must go back to Brooklyn.
Why should we have an American over here telling us what to do?
No disrespect, but the talks were a waste of time.
Pack your bags and go home.
It's a farce.

Professor Meghan O'Sullivan refused to be dispirited. True there was a bit of a death rattle over the flag business and that would be put on hold in the meantime, but after they had grafted over the fourth draft she assured him that the past and the parades issues might be sorted out.

Meghan O'Sullivan's last statement after the crunch talks failed to produce any resolution was: 'We don't think that it's time for a post-mortem. This isn't dead in the water – there's still a lot of potential life left in the agreement.' Richard was so keen to have his proposals accepted that he almost willed the parties to agree. This would have been the best Christmas box that a troubled people could have wished for – like children waking up on Christmas morning they would have pulled off the wrapping and found a balm for their woes and an exorcist for their troubled demons. He wasn't looking for another medal like the one he got for his work during Operation Desert Shield and Operation Desert Storm. He was just looking for a resolution to the talks.

Will he come back again?
Perhaps, perhaps …

I must admit I have been a bit over the top and *Curious Incident of the Dog in the Night-Time*sque about my research, but I never do things by half. I hope I have been objective in carrying out my project – I don't think autistic people are capable of bias. I think I have consulted as many sources as possible, and, after all, I was born on the very day the Agreement was signed and that must count for something. An autistic person has special gifts – a bit like Salman Rushdie's character Saleem Sinai having special powers. I know I wasn't born at midnight where 'clock-hands joined palms in respectful greeting'. No, my entry into the world was not as auspicious as that of Saleem's, nor did my mother go to a soothsayer while she was pregnant – but she did say that when she was a teenager a fortune teller told her she would marry a wealthy man, live by the sea and have three children. In *Midnight's Children* Ramram Seth provided Saleem's mother with the following prediction:

> A son ... such a son! ... A son, Sahiba, who will never be older than his motherland – neither older nor younger ... There will be two heads – but you shall see only one – there will be knees and a nose, a nose and knees ... Newspaper praises him, two mothers raise him! Bicyclists love him – but, crowds will shove him! Sisters will weep; cobra will creep ... Washing will hide him – voices will guide him! Friends mutilate him – blood will betray him! Spittoons will brain him – doctors will drain him – jungle will claim him – wizards reclaim him! Soldiers will try him – tyrants will fry him ... He will have sons without having sons! He will be old before he is old! *And he will die ... before he is dead!*

Nor was I, to my knowledge, switched at birth by a crazy midwife in the maternity unit – you couldn't get away with it these days; in *Midnight's Children* Mary Pereira switched Shiva and Saleem at birth in order to impress her sweetheart Joseph D'Costa. No, I was no changeling, but I still think I have a special destiny. Since there was no Ramram Seth to predict my fortune, I have availed of an online astrology website called Cosmic Navigator to furnish me with an astrology report:

Name: Patrick Sweeney
Born: April 10 1998 3:00 PM
Time Zone: BST Belfast, UK

Rising Sign is in 28 Degrees Leo.
You love to be the centre of attention. Try not to be such a show off!

Sun is in 20 Degrees Aries.
You are an enthusiastic leader but you tend to be a reluctant follower.

Moon is in 05 Degrees Libra.
Unpleasantness should be avoided at all costs. You are uncomfortable with strangers but at ease and sociable with friends and associates.

Mercury is in 13 Degrees Aries.
Very quick-witted. An independent thinker.

Venus is in 04 Degrees Pisces.
You have a dreamy, fanciful, romantic nature. A very creative imagination.

Mars is in 28 Degrees Aries.
At times, in your zeal to get ahead, you are tactless and offensive.

Jupiter is in 15 Degrees Pisces.

You are at your best when you give of yourself. Try to avoid being a martyr.

Saturn is in 22 Degrees Aries.
You are aloof, independent, standoffish.

Uranus is in 12 Degrees Aquarius.
You, and most of your peer group, are reformers at heart. You want to make positive changes that will benefit society as a whole.

Neptune is in 02 Degrees Aquarius.
You and your entire generation will idealise and even venerate the ability to remain detached as well as the ability to objectively analyse any given situation. There will be a concerted effort on your part to cure the ills of society as a whole.

Pluto is in 07 Degrees Sagittarius.
For your entire generation, society's cherished belief totems will be radically changed.
Many traditional concepts will be totally altered if not completely destroyed. The rights of individuals to pursue their own course in life will be reasserted.

North Node is in 10 Degrees Virgo.
Usually quite unselfish, you will toil long hours in the service of any worthy cause that
demands your attention.

Tony Blair was right when he said the hand of history was on our shoulders the day the Agreement was signed. People had such high expectations when the Agreement was endorsed, but many were not aware that the hardest part of the journey was yet to be travelled. Amela Puljek-Shank highlighted the strength and inner courage that is required to heal:

> To take the road of healing is very difficult and it requires courage and strength to carry the process through. During this time we need support, love, and understanding of those who are closest to us. We need people to support us in this process.

I emerged into daylight just the way the Agreement did. The Agreement was to herald a new period of peace and understanding and the principle of consent was enshrined in the new deal: if the majority wished to remain in Britain, they would have their wishes respected – the IRA would no longer use violence to bring about a United Ireland.

A new era of cooperation was ushered in. When the politicians emerged there was a tangible sense of emotion. It was like a birth, and there was so much expectation.

Even when the midnight children come together purpose is still a problem. Saleem and Shiva argue about it constantly:

> The thing is, we must be here for a *purpose*, don't you think? I mean, there has to be a *reason*, you must agree? So what I thought, we should try and work out what it is, and then, you know, sort of dedicate our lives to ...

I have so much in common with Saleem that it almost overwhelms me. He felt that he and the other midnight children had a special mission to fulfil even though they were not clear what exactly it was. Although he doesn't know that he's a changeling at the beginning of the book or that his biological father was an Englishman, making him Anglo-Indian, he still felt the hand of destiny upon him:

I must work fast, faster that Scheherazade, if I am to end up meaning – yes, meaning – something. I admit it: above all things, I fear absurdity.

I feel my calling is no less urgent than Saleem's now that I've delved into the history of my birth and how it coincided with the signing of the Agreement. I did use an online tool, which sounds somewhat prosaic compared to the inscrutable Shri Ramram Seth in Rushdie's book – but the world evolves, and who's to say a Cosmic Navigator astrological reading is not just as valid as one from an enigmatic Indian seer. I'm amazed that Neptune was in the 02 Degrees Aquarius configuration which stated, 'There will be a concerted effort on your part to cure the ills of society as a whole'. Surely this prophesy can't be a random line churned out from a website? I have to make a difference. I have to cure the ills of my nation. After carrying out my research I am excited by the prospect of such a mission, but, at the same time, I quake at the enormity of the task – I'm not overly optimistic about power-sharing in the Assembly.

I find parallels between Saleem and myself. He was born into a post-independence India which was partitioned into two separate countries a short time after the British left – the Union of India, which was predominantly Hindu, and the Dominion of Pakistan, which was mostly Muslim. The British withdrawal didn't bring about an era of peace. On the contrary, the country was plunged into chaos, and ethnic and religious conflict was rampant; Mahatma Gandhi, the leader of the freedom movement, was assassinated on 30 January 1948. I was born at the introduction of a devolved Assembly into a country that was already partitioned. Of course I must acknowledge that the province I was born into was relatively peaceful after the Agreement had been signed, but it was more of an armed peace.

Line in the Sand

Victim's Testimony

They're nowhere near it.

Nowhere near sorting
Out the ordinary people's cases
So they're not!

My brother was walking home from
Work
So he was!

Gunmen shot him dead and dumped
His body in waste ground
So they did!

I was seventeen years old
So I was!

They're only doing the high profile cases
So they are!

People haven't got over these things
So they haven't

My sister breaks her heart every day
So she does!

You can't go on with the future
Until the past is sorted out

So you can't

Peace is Rough

Should a line be drawn in the sand? Will it be a squiggly line? I wonder how the legacy of the past can be dealt with.

The UVF took collective responsibility for their part in the Troubles. The IRA disbanded and therefore cannot bear witness. Those who signed up to the Good Friday Agreement cannot give evidence – the government doesn't want to be embarrassed. So, how do we deal with the murky stuff of the past? Some people don't want to hear about the past, so, in a way, there can be no definitive closure. It's a false dawn for the victims if they can't get closure.

It's said that even if we try to ignore the past, the past will not ignore us – it's like an incurable hangover which recurs every day. Every day that we open a newspaper a Troubles story has been resurrected to be dissected once more: it might be an unsolved murder, an appeal for information or the discovery of the body of one of the Disappeared, an inquest. One of the stories that got a lot of media coverage was the appointment of a former IRA member to the position of special adviser in the new Assembly in 2011. She had been involved in the murder of a young female school teacher outside a Catholic Church in South Belfast.

The Ulster Unionist Party issued a position paper, *Dealing with the Past*:

> The failure to address the past is often cited as the Achilles Heel of devolution; some argue we cannot achieve a better, cohesive, shared future without first dealing with our past.

The paper goes on to argue that our methods for dealing with the legacy of the past are inadequate and that '… we have a set of mechanisms that are imperfect, incomplete and imbalanced'. In *Macbeth* Macbeth says to the three witches, 'Stay, you imperfect speakers: tell me more.' The Agreement, like the witches' prophesies, seemed to herald so much, and yet their predictions were flawed from the beginning. Macbeth took the witches' riddles at face value not realising that they weren't cast-iron guarantees granting him invincibility. The witches predicted that Macbeth would be king. To achieve this he commits regicide and then goes on a murderous spree in order to copper-fasten his kingdom all the while assured by the witches that he is invincible as according to them no man born of woman can overpower him. Macbeth later learns that Macduff was born by Caesarean section therefore rendering him vulnerable.

Bernard S. Mayer wrote:

> [Humans] are very imperfect communicators. Sometimes this imperfection generates conflict, whether or not there is a significant incompatibility of interests, and it almost always makes conflict harder to deal with effectively.

In his practitioner's guide to the dynamics of conflict resolution he spoke of the cognitive, emotional and behavioural dimensions of conflict. Because of these dimensions, conflict resolution can be a complex business. Sometimes a peace accord can provide space to negotiate a true and lasting peace. For example, after he signed the treaty document drawn up by the British Government in 1921, Michael Collins remarked that the treaty gave Ireland 'the freedom to achieve freedom'. Unfortunately that treaty ended the war with Britain but started the civil war as brother fought brother and the country was split down the middle. Collins and his negotiating team had plenipotentiary powers to sign the treaty. A plenipotentiary is defined in the dictionary as a:

> A person, especially a diplomat, invested with the full power of independent action on behalf of their government, typically in a foreign country.

So the treaty that ended British rule in the twenty-six counties sparked off a bloody civil war, and one of the leaders of the negotiating team was shot by one of his own people. Ironically, then, a treaty or an agreement can open up new challenges. An American-Palestinian poet, Naomi Shihab Nye, wrote a poem about a young man she met on the bus a few hours after the tragedy of 9/11. Here is an excerpt of it:

Flinn, On the Bus

> Flinn looked at his free hands
> more than the fields,
> turned them over in his lap,
> 'no snap judgments, no quick angers,
> I'll stand back, look at what happens,
> think calmly what my next step should be.'
> It was not hard to nod,
> to wish him well. But could I tell
> what had happened in the world
> on his long-awaited day,
> what twists of rage greater
> than we could ever guess
> had savaged skylines, thousands of lives?
> I could not. He'd find out
> soon enough. Flinn, take it easy.
> Peace is rough.

Naomi's poem would be an excellent manifesto for post-conflict societies. We should 'stand back, look at what happens, [and] think calmly what … [the] next step should be'.

I have decided to use the Irish version of my name and henceforth I will refer to myself as Pádraig Mac Suibhne. Pádraig comes from the Latin name *Patricius* which means 'nobleman'.

> Variants: Pádraic, Pádraig
> Diminutives: Paddy, Patsy, Pat
> Other Languages:
> Breton: Padrig
> French: Patrice
> German: Patricia
> Croatian: Patrik
> Czech: Patrik
> Hungarian: Patrik
> Italian: Patrizio
> Manx: Pherick
> Maori: Patariki
> Medieval English: Pate
> Polish: Patryk
> Portugese: Patrício
> Slovak: Patrik
> Spanish: Patricio
> Swedish: Patrik
> Welsh: Padrig

Fictional representations include Lord Harry, known as Patrick, from *The Railway Series* by Rev W. Awdry, Patrick Bateman, from Bret Easton Ellis' *American Psycho*, Sir Patrick Delaney-Podmore, from *Harry Potter* and Patrick Star, from SpongeBob SquarePants, a television series.

'Son of the pleasant one'

Sweeney or Mac Suibhne means 'son of Suibhne'. It is said to be of Scottish origin and means, 'pleasant' or 'well-disposed'.

Fictional representations include Sweeney, from T.S. Eliot's *Sweeney Agonistes*, Sweeney Todd, the serial killer, Lieutenant Sweeney, from the film *Dead Men Walking* and Mad Sweeney from Seamus Heaney's *Sweeney Astray*.

I am honoured that poets as famous and prolific as Eliot and Heaney have used my surname in their literary creations. Eliot's *Sweeney Agonistes: Fragments of an Aristophanic Melodrama* was an experimental verse drama and was written in a music-hall style with songs and short scenes. It was a commentary on the emptiness and hollowness of modern life.

Tantalus, son of Zeus, summoned the gods to a great feast where he served up pieces of his mutilated son, Pelops, in a dish. This was hardly a dish for the gods, and, of course, they spurned his offering. But one of the gods, Demeter, accidently ate a piece of Pelops which turned out to be his shoulder. Tantalus was subsequently banished to the underworld where he stands for all eternity in a pool where food and water are just out of his reach, thus tantalising him but never satisfying his hunger. Pelops, who was put back together by the gods meanwhile, cheated in a chariot race to win the hand of Hippodameia, Oenomaus's daughter. He was cursed by Myrtilus, the charioteer whom he cheated and murdered, and then Atreus, son of Pelops, was cursed for fratricide and dismembering his nephews and cooking them for main course. Aegisthus, a product of Thyestes and his daughter Pelopia, murdered Atreus and put his father back on the throne. So you might say that Orestes' ancestors committed murders most horrid and his family tree was tainted by unimaginable homicides and acts of cannibalism.

Their deeds brought curses and the family was plagued with misfortune. So, in essence, we have murder, incest and treachery in Greek history, and these murderous characters never get away with it; they pay the price of their deeds over the years as the gods wreak their vengeance.

The epigraph below is from Choephori, the second play from *The Oresteia* trilogy, which was written by an ancient Greek playwright, Aeschylus. In the play Orestes is pursued by the avenging Furies or Erinyes, deities from the underworld, who are hunting him because he murdered his mother, Clytemnestra, who had previously murdered her husband, Agamemnon, because he had sacrificed their daughter, Iphigenia, to appease the gods. Agamemnon sacrificed his daughter because he had a killed a deer which was held sacred by Artemis. The latter becalmed the seas preventing Agamemnon's ships from returning to Troy. The prophet Calchas said that Iphigenia's death was the only thing that could appease Artemis.

Ultimately Orestes is cursed for matricide and is hunted by the harpies:

> Orestes: You don't see them, you don't – but I see them: they are hunting me down, I must move on.

But he also atones for the sins of his ancestors through the intervention of Athena: like the negotiators in the Good Friday Agreement she hammered out a compromise that was acceptable to both sides. She appealed to Apollo's masculinity and to the Furies and agreed a power-sharing deal with them regarding Athens. Nobody really got what they wanted, but by couching her arguments in paradoxical language she avoided moral absolutes, and Orestes was no longer hounded and tormented by the Furies. As Peter Levi comments:

> A tragedy is played out,
> a curse is reversed,
> natural order is restored,
> a family saga unfolds,

T.S. Eliot's Sweeney has committed some terrible crime although he doesn't acknowledge it is him who has carried out the heinous crime.

> I knew a man once did a girl in.
> Any man might do a girl in
> Any man has to, needs to, wants to
> Once in a lifetime, do a girl in.

Sweeney is tormented and the Full Chorus of Mr Klipstein, Mr Krumpacker, Captain Horsfall and Mr Wauchope describe this nightmarish landscape:

> You've had a cream of a nightmare dream and you've got
> the hoo-ha's [terror, dread] coming to you.

The Greeks believed that the gods punished and rewarded humans according to their deeds:

> Fate was forceful
> Chance was perverse
> Oracles were capricious
> Zeus was vindictive
> The odds were never in our favour
> The Gods were fickle

Seamus Heaney's *Sweeney Astray* was a translation of *Buile Suibhne*, a medieval Irish text. The hero of *Buile Suibhne* was Mad Sweeney, son of Colman Cuar, King of Dal-Arie, an outcast poet-king who was turned into a mad flying creature after a run-in with a local saint. He became a pariah finding no rest or sanctuary in the world:

> I am Sweeney, the whinger,
> the scuttler in the valley.
> But call me instead,
> Peak-pate, Stag-head.

The springs I always liked
were the one at Dunmall
and the well on Knocklayde
that tasted pure and cool.

Mendicant forever
Frayed, scant and raggedy
high in the mountains
like a crazed, frost bitten sentry

I find no bed, no quarter,
no place in the sun –
not even in this reddening
covert of tall fern.

Moling, a good priest, helps Sweeney to regain his sanity. He speaks these words at the end:

Because Mad Sweeney was a pilgrim
to the lip of every well
and every green-banked, cress-topped stream,
their water's his memorial.

Now, if it be the will of God,
rise, Sweeney, take this guiding hand
that has to lay you in the sod
and draw the dark blinds of the ground.

I ask a blessing, by Sweeney's grave
His memory flutters in my breast.
His soul roosts in the tree of love.
His body sinks in its clay nest.

The epigraph below comes from St John of the Cross in *Ascent of Mount Carmel*, a book on Christian mysticism. St John of the Cross was a famous Spanish poet who described the journey of the soul to God as a profound struggle in the quest to achieve unity with the divine.

> Hence the soul cannot be possessed of the divine union, until it has divested itself of the love of created beings.

To achieve union with God the soul must journey away from people and face a terrible dark night:

> In a dark night
> With longings kindled in love
> oh blessed chance
> I went forth without being observed
> My house already being at rest
> Through darkness and secure
> By the secret ladder disguised
> oh blessed chance
> Through darkness and in concealment
> My house already being at rest

It is estimated that there are ninety-nine peace walls in Belfast. The first peace wall was erected in 1969 and was seen as a short-term course of action during the serious rioting that had broken out in Belfast. A British Army Major commented, 'This is a temporary measure,' and added, 'We do not want to see another Berlin wall situation in Western Europe ... it will be gone by Christmas.' Now they are more or less a permanent feature of the city. Sometimes the walls are known as peace lines; the longest of which is in West Belfast and separates the Catholic Falls Road from the Protestant Shankill Road. This wall, Cupar Way peace wall, is forty-five feet high and eight hundred and seventy-five yards long and is topped by barbed wire. There are forty-four walls in north Belfast, thirty in west Belfast, fourteen in the centre of the town, ten in east Belfast and one in south Belfast.

John Paul Lederach commented that 'human security is not tied primarily to the quantity or size of weapons, the height or thickness of the wall that separates them, nor to the power of imposition or control'. So, how can we get rid of the walls? How can we have a city without walls? As the Community Relations Council (CRC) comments:

> The barriers separate communities in which the fear remains that, without the barrier, lives will be put at risk. They freeze the geography and demography of single-identity communities and prevent all sorts of normal freedom of movement.

I suppose the walls create a certain amount of security, but at the same time their presence highlights the fact that things are not normal, and they are a blot on the landscape. Undoubtedly the city has been transformed – you only have to visit Victoria Square with its upmarket stores and CastleCourt with its many successful businesses, the centre of Belfast with all its new cafés and restaurants, and you would see that we are experiencing regeneration.

A few years ago I saw a couple dancing outside CastleCourt; it was wonderful that Belfast was stable enough to have a couple dancing in the street rather than diving for cover after a bomb warning. I am so sorry for those who are not able, for one reason or another, to celebrate how far we've come. Senator Mitchell's son commented that Stormont was boring – Senator Mitchell said boring is good, bombing is bad.

Share Space

I got the definition of 'share' from an online etymology site:

> Share: Old English *scearu* 'a cutting, shearing, tonsure; a part or division' related to *sceran* 'to cut' from Proto-Germanic *skaro-* (cognates: Old High German *scara* 'troop, share of forced labour' German *Schar* 'troop, band' properly 'a part of an army' Old Norse *skör* 'rim').

> Some people want their share.
> Some people want the lion's share.
> Some people want to buy shares.
> Some people want to share and share alike.
> Some people want to turn swords into ploughshares.

> Space: 'extent or area; room' (to do something), a shortening of Old French *espace* 'period of time, distance, interval', from Latin *spatium* 'room, area, distance, stretch of time' of unknown origin (also source of Spanish *espacio*, Italian *spazio*).

> Some people want their own space.
> Some people want a parking space.
> Some people like the open space.
> Some kids like Myspace.
> Some people have gone to outer space.

In Ireland we try to share space.

> By faith the walls of Jericho fell down, after they were compassed about seven days.

I am also reminded of Robert Frost's poem *Mending Wall*.

Good Friday's Child and the Good Friday Agreement

Something there is that doesn't love a wall,
That sends the frozen-ground-swell under it,
And spills the upper boulders in the sun;
And makes gaps even two can pass abreast.
The work of hunters is another thing:
I have come after them and made repair
Where they have left not one stone on a stone,
But they would have the rabbit out of hiding,
To please the yelping dogs. The gaps I mean,
No one has seen them made or heard them made,
But at spring mending-time we find them there.
I let my neighbour know beyond the hill;
And on a day we meet to walk the line
And set the wall between us once again.
We keep the wall between us as we go.
To each the boulders that have fallen to each.
And some are loaves and some so nearly balls
We have to use a spell to make them balance:
'Stay where you are until our backs are turned!'
We wear our fingers rough with handling them.
Oh, just another kind of out-door game,
One on a side. It comes to little more:
There where it is we do not need the wall:
He is all pine and I am apple orchard.
My apple trees will never get across
And eat the cones under his pines, I tell him.
He only says, 'Good fences make good neighbours.'
Spring is the mischief in me, and I wonder
If I could put a notion in his head:
'*Why* do they make good neighbours? Isn't it
Where there are cows? But here there are no cows.
Before I built a wall I'd ask to know
What I was walling in or walling out,

> And to whom I was like to give offence.
> Something there is that doesn't love a wall,
> That wants it down.' I could say 'Elves' to him,
> But it's not elves exactly, and I'd rather
> He said it for himself. I see him there
> Bringing a stone grasped firmly by the top
> In each hand, like an old-stone savage armed.
> He moves in darkness as it seems to me,
> Not of woods only and the shade of trees.
> He will not go behind his father's saying,
> And he likes having thought of it so well
> He says again, 'Good fences make good neighbours.'

It's not so easy to tear down a deeply held belief among humankind that they need walls between them. In ancient Roman times there was a celebration known as Terminalia which was a festival to worship Terminus, the god who protected boundary markers. The terminus or boundary stones were evidence of the outer limits of ancient Rome, and every year on 23 February the stones on each side would be festooned with flowers, and a religious ceremony took place which included sprinkling the stones with blood. So the need to establish boundaries goes back many thousand years, and I can understand why people would want to establish boundaries to ascertain the outer limits of a city, but I fail to see how this works within a city. Belfast is a small city where Protestants and Catholics live cheek-by-jowl; a stone's throw from each and yet they don't interact, and the Troubles brought about even greater segregation. As Darby points out, the two sides avoided contact if possible but if not, interactions were short and sweet.

A wall separating East Berlin from the west of the city was erected in 1961 and was taken down in 1989. Willy Brandt, the former chancellor of Germany, referred to it as the 'Wall of Shame'.

The Berlin Wall

Wire
Meshing
Anti-vehicle
Trenches
Concrete
Slabs
Stony
Faces
Checkpoint
Charlie
Cold
War
Surveillance
Patrol
Car
Searches
Barbed
Wire
Escape
Attempts
Guenter
Litfin
Chris
Gueffroy

Wall woodpeckers came with hammers to chisel chunks for souvenirs – perhaps to keep or sell. Some segments ended up in hotels.

One thousand plastic-foam dominoes painted by children were toppled to commemorate the twentieth anniversary of the fall of the infamous wall. The first giant block was toppled by Lech Wałęsa, a former Polish president. There is no East; no West.

Devolution Talks

Hard going at Hillsborough
Hailstones beat on the windowpane.

Hillsborough again.
Another deadline,
another lockdown,
another countdown.

Mr Robinson said he
was 'not interested
in deadlines.
If the deal isn't right
it won't be done,' he said.

Mr Durkan said
'We have had
the outbursts here
we need outcomes.'

Mr Brown went
back to London and
Mr Cowan to Dublin
without a deal.

Hilary Clinton sent a message
Of encouragement.
Brown says if they cannot agree,
he will force their hand.
He will give an ultimatum.

So in ancient Rome boundary markers were celebrated; in modern Europe the tearing down of the Berlin Wall was a matter for rejoicing, and each year the anniversary of its demolition is celebrated. But in Belfast the walls are still there, an ugly reminder of the breakdown of the peace process. Maybe the peace is going to be piecemeal.

There are thirteen clusters of peace walls in Belfast:

> Suffolk–Lenadoon
> Upper Springfield Road
> Falls–Shankill
> The Village–Westlink
> Inner Ring
> Duncairn Gardens
> Limestone Road–Alexandra Park
> Lower Oldpark–Manor Street
> Crumlin Road–Ardoyne–Glenbryn
> Ligoniel
> Whitewell Road–Longlands
> Short Strand–Inner East
> Ormeau Road and the Markets

I took the first letter of each cluster and was able to make a three-word mnemonic:

> Sculls Wild Oft

Ciaran Carson wrote a poem entitled *Peace*

> Back then you wouldn't know from one day to the next what might
> happen next. Everything was, as it were, provisional, slipping from the unforeseeable into tomorrow even as the jittery present became history.

> The Indian writer, looking back at India, does so through guilt-tinted spectacles. ... I am speaking now of those of us who emigrated, and I suspect that there are times when the move seems wrong to us all, when we seem, to ourselves, post-lapsarian men and women. We are Hindus who have crossed the black water; we are Muslims who eat pork. And as a result – as my use of the Christian notion of the fall indicates – we are now partly of the West. Our identity is at once plural and partial. Sometimes we feel that we straddle two cultures; at other times, we fall between two stools ...
>
> (Rushdie)

> After decades of separation and no common institutions the two (or more) peoples' relationships, some of the core conflict issues, the attitudes towards war as a means to resolve conflict, peacebuilding capacity and other characteristics of the conflict system are very different from the initial constellation of the above characteristics.
>
> (Ropers)

> Civil society has the capacity to develop 'peripheral vision', or 'the capacity to situate oneself in a changing environment with a sense of direction and purpose and at the same time

develop an ability to see and move with the unexpected … With the peripheral vision change processes have a flexible strength, never find dead ends that stop their movement, and relish complexity precisely because complexity never stops offering up new things that may create ways forward, around, or behind whatever jumps in the way.

(Lederach)

Postscript or Epilogue: It's Not a Post-Mortem

I was seventeen on 10 April 2015. I grew up with the Agreement which was the culmination of many agreements. I didn't get a good start and I've had to face many challenges. Most boys my age have a girlfriend or have been in relationships. I do have feelings only I find it difficult to express them. Most boys my age hang out in the town centre and give their parents cheek and their teachers gyp. Most boys my age don't want to be seen out with their parents. Most boys my age have experimented with drink and drugs. One of the boys, Ivan, was even suspended for smoking weed. He didn't know how to follow the rules. He was a boy from a wealthy family and I thought he had everything. He would tell everyone about his foreign holidays and about where he was off to next. I could see him passing his driving test and having a really cool car and lots of girlfriends. He seemed to live in an impenetrable castle of privileges yet he became a real troublemaker, always challenging his teachers and never having his homework done.

The Agreement had had a stormy birth and never really hit the ground running. The Agreement was like the boy in my class, Ivan, who was style over substance. This morning Mike Nesbitt, the only Unionist MLA, withdrew from the Assembly as he and his party were unhappy about the recent murder of Kevin McGuigan in August 2015 in East Belfast and the alleged IRA involvement.

> Mike Nesbitt said
> The two main parties are a sham.
> The Assembly is hanging by a thread.

> The Chief Constable says the IRA has not gone away
> But he accepted the bona fides of the Sinn Féin that
> They had rejected.

> There was a firewall around the Sinn Féin
> Leaders, but in reality the rank-and-file
> IRA members were there carrying out murders.
> Mo Mowlan, a former Secretary, said there would
> Be some internal housekeeping to be done with the
> IRA. Perhaps an informer needed taken out.
> Gerry Adams says the IRA has gone away.
> The trust has gone.
> Mike Nesbitt says it's the right thing to do.
> He said the DUP and Sinn Féin have failed abysmally.
> Sinn Féin talked the talk, but had they walked the walk?
> We need to rebuild the vision of 1998.

Lord Alderdice's Advice.

> Lord Alderdice says the guns are decommissioned,
> But the IRA has not been disbanded or diminished
> The structures are still there.

They are still intact.
He has suggested the IMC should not be reinstated. Just because the symptoms are the same, it does not mean that the same treatment would work this time.

The IMC stands for the Independent Monitoring Commission. According to Dáil Éireann's Aengus Ó Snodaigh the IMC consisted of 'three spooks and a Lord' in tow.

The IMC's remit was to:

1. Monitor any paramilitary activity
2. Monitor the British Government's security normalisation process
3. Handle claims that a minister or party is not committed to peace

In its lifetime it published twenty-two reports, including three ad hoc reports.

> Imperfect peace in Northern Ireland must be repaired.
> This is not a game of musical chairs. We don't need
> Any more déjà vu. Enough fudging and stalling.
> Enough talking shops and pseudo-politics.
> Enough whataboutery
> Is this as good as it gets? Are we condemned
> To ceaseless impasses? Are we just like Sisyphus
> Cursed for all eternity to roll a boulder up a
> Hill just to have it come crashing down again?
> Will it always be a logjam, a stalemate?

> Humpty Dumpty sat on a wall.
> Humpty Dumpty had a great fall.

All the king's horses and all the king's men
Couldn't put Humpty together again.

The IMC was made up of Lord Alderdice, former Alliance Party leader, former Speaker of the Northern Ireland Assembly and current peer in the British House of Lords; Joe Brosnan, former Secretary General of the Department of Justice in the Republic; John Grieve, former Deputy Assistant Commissioner of the Metropolitan Police and former head of the Metropolitan Police Anti-Terror Branch; and Dick Kerr, former deputy director of the CIA. Brosnan, Grieve and Kerr were the three spooks that Aengus Ó Snodaigh referred to.

The Peace Process: The Fresh Process
But Sisyphean Stormont will meet again and the MLAs will roll that boulder up the Stormont hill once more. Representatives will come across the sea from London, and representatives from the Irish government will cross the border and descend on it. Senator Gary Hart, the US special envoy to Northern Ireland, will urge all the parties to engage in constructive politics. Apparently America is 'disproportionately interested' in NI politics. They have no self-interest whatsoever. They will say the scope has widened and that there is room for more trade-offs. Hart is not Haas; this is not horse-trading. They say they will be sensitive and discreet. The British government will threaten to close down the Assembly and reinstate direct rule. That is their prerogative. That is the last card they want to play, so they say, the last road they want to go down, so they proclaim, they say their hands are tied – however, their tongues are not. If the Assembly cannot get it together and deliver on the Welfare Reform Bill, it will be done over their heads, taken out of their hands, and everyone will say they have done their best, that they cannot do any more, that the murder of Kevin McGuigan was a bridge too far, a deal-breaker, *la paille finale*.

And then Peter Robinson will announce that there will be no further meeting of the Northern Ireland Executive unless there are exceptional circumstances. He will say their party cannot be expected to continue as if nothing had happened. He will say that it cannot be business as usual. He will announce that there will be no more North/South Ministerial meetings in any format. He will say that unless we get to the bottom of this recent crisis, the peace process will not be seen as a shining example of peace but a cautionary tale of stopping and starting, of dilly-dallying. He will say that.

Mike Nesbitt, Ulster Unionist Party, will say that the Democratic Unionist Party are confused and are playing the hokey-cokey:

> You put your right foot in,
> Your right foot out,
> in, out, in, out
> You shake it all about.
> You do the hokey-cokey,
> And you turn around,
> That's what it's all about …

They will say that this will be the first day in the history of Northern Ireland's parliament that the Assembly has met without the Unionist Party. Mike Nesbitt will say that Sinn Féin and the PSNI need to be on the same page regarding the status of the IRA. He will say that Stormont has become dysfunctional and the stitch-up has become a face-off.

Jim Allister, Traditional Unionist Voice leader, will say that the Agreement was just a sticking plaster and that we need root-and-branch change. He deplores the mandatory coalition and its crippling mutual vetoes.

Sinn Féin will say the IRA has gone away. Deputy First Minister Martin McGuinness will say that, 'The people who murdered Jock

Davison are criminals. Those who murdered Kevin McGuigan are also criminals. They must be brought to justice.' Gerry Kelly, Sinn Féin, will say: 'Sinn Féin has called consistently on people to support the PSNI investigations into the killings of Kevin McGuigan and Gerard Davison.' Gerry Kelly will say that the Chief Constable George Hamilton's statement was contradictory.

In *The Book: On the Taboo Against Knowing Who You Are* Alan Watts spoke of the social double bind game – a kind of damned if you do and damned if you don't game:

> The first rule of this game is that it is not a game.
> Everyone must play.
> You must love us.
> You must go on living.
> Be yourself, but play a consistent and acceptable role.
> Control yourself and be natural.
> Try to be sincere.

The Assembly's first rule is that it is not an Assembly.

> Everyone must play.
> Everyone must not play.
> Everyone must go away.
> Everyone must not go away.
> Everyone must go on making decisions.
> Everyone must stop making decisions.
> Everyone must be sincere.
> Everyone must be insincere.
> Everyone must be on the one page.
> Everyone must not be on the one page.
> Everyone must be kicked out.
> Everyone must not be kicked out.
> Everyone must sort out the Welfare Reform Bill.

Everyone must not sort out the Welfare Reform Bill.
Everyone must pull the plug.
Everyone must not pull the plug.
Everyone said Stormont was dysfunctional.
Everyone said Stormont was not dysfunctional.
Everyone said power-sharing should be collapsed.
Everyone said power-sharing should not be collapsed.
Everyone said that the IRA has left the stage.
Everyone said that the IRA has not left the stage.
Everyone said that the IRA has left the theatre.
Everyone said that the IRA has not left the theatre.
Everyone said there should be an adjournment.
Everyone said there should not be an adjournment.
Everyone said there should be a suspension.
Everyone said there should not be a suspension.
Everyone said the cat's out of the bag.
Everyone said the cat's not out of the bag.
Everyone says we should give Sinn Féin the benefit of the doubt.
Everyone says we should not give Sinn Féin the benefit of the doubt.
Everyone says we should give Sinn Féin the time of day.
Everyone says we should not give Sinn Féin the time of day.
Everyone will say Sinn Féin should step up to the plate.
Everyone will say Sinn Féin should not step up to the plate.
Everyone will say Stormont has failed.
Everyone will say Stormont has not failed.
Everyone said it was on the cards.
Everyone said it was not on the cards.
Everyone said we need to buy time.
Everyone said we do not need to buy time.

Whataboutery: what about this? What about that?
What about this atrocity, this tit for tat?
What about a tooth for a tooth?
What about an eye for an eye?
What about like for like?
What about measure for measure?
What about *lex talionis*?
What about retaliation?
What about the La Mon restaurant bombing?
What about the Miami Showband massacre?
What about Bloody Sunday?
What about Bloody Friday?
What about the Poppy Day massacre?
What about the Ballymurphy massacre?
What about the Kingsmill massacre?
What about the Loughinisland massacre?
What about the Darkley Gospel Hall massacre?
What about the Castlerock killings?
What about the Greysteel massacre?
What about the Shankill Road bombing?
What about the killing of Jock Davison?
What about the murder of Kevin McGuigan?
What about the Plantation?
What about the Union flag dispute?
What about the parades?
What about the Parades Commission?
What about the Parades Commission's determinations?
What about contentious parades?
What about route restrictions?
What about the 1916 commemorations?
What about Camp Twaddell?

What about Garvaghy Road?
What about the past?
What about the victims of violence?
What about the Historical Enquiries Team?
What about the Boston secret tapes?
What about the Bloody Sunday Inquiry?
What about the Milltown Cemetery killings?
What about the mother of ten who disappeared?
What about the Disappeared?
What about the Independent Commission for the Location of Victims' Remains?
What about the unsolved murders?

In *The Thick of It*! The clock is ticking. This is high-stakes, high-risks. This is not a game of snap. This crisis feels familiar. We are close to the brink. We are into injury time. We are on our last legs. It is do-or-die, last gasp, last chance saloon. The Agreement is on life support. The loveless marriage is over. The two sides only stayed together because of their electorate. We had a fantasy budget, and now we have a zombie assembly. It's like an episode from *Dr Who* – we are in science fiction mode and all we need now is the Tardis. And Stephen Nolan, who has the biggest show in the country, lives on fantasy island. Some are saying that failure was on the cards, some are saying that Sinn Féin wants to be in the mandatory coalition but that the Unionists had to be in it, and as in any forced marriage, tensions can emerge.

Harold Good, a witness at decommissioning, will say pull back from the brink because it will be hard to get this back. Harold Good will urge the politicians not to be too hasty. He will also say that we are not in a post-conflict situation, we are only emerging from conflict.

Breaking news:

This morning three leading Republicans were arrested. They are being questioned at Antrim Police Station. Their names are Eddie Copeland, Bobby Storey and Brian Gillen.

Michael McDowell, former Minister for Justice, will say that it would be better if the IRA becomes an 'unarmed and withering husk' rather than turning into a hardened husk with claws sharpened.

Mike Nesbitt will call for a suspension of the Assembly. Peter Robinson and the DUP will call for an adjournment. An adjournment would mean that up to a point it would be business as usual for the ministers – they would carry on with their meetings and they would still get paid.

De Chastelain said that not every gun was accounted for at the end of decommissioning.

But all this political analysing has made me forget to mention that I failed my GSCE English for the second time. Even after all the research I carried out for my teacher, I still failed. She said I was only supposed to carry out a piece of research and pick out the main points of the Good Friday Agreement – that the idea was to garner enough information in order to generate a group discussion. She said that knowledge of the topic was important for chairing the discussion but not encyclopedic knowledge. She said other things were needed to chair a discussion, for example being able to keep a discussion on track, being able to listen to contributions made, being able to make suggestions and being able to sum it all up at the end. So basically I got a D for the speaking and listening part of my exam. As for the role-play part, it was the most absurd thing I ever had to do in my life – why would you want to pretend to be another person? I had to pretend to be a WWI soldier who thought that the war was going to be over by Christmas and who thought that being a soldier was all about girls and cigarettes. On my first night in the trenches my commanding officer, Nick, who was playing the role of Wilfred Owen, the war poet, tries to put me right. It all leads to him pulling a poem out of his pocket entitled *Anthem for Doomed Youth* so that the scales fell from my eyes. It was so hard to imagine that Nick could ever be a poet – he hates poetry! As for my talk, apparently I didn't make eye contact with the class. Anyone who knows anything about autism knows that sufferers do not like making any kind of contact, including eye contact!

The British government isn't going to rush in to save Stormont. There are no helicopters hovering on the lawn, no big guns are going to sort it all out. David Cameron says he is 'extremely worried'. But not worried enough to forgo a cricket match. Yes, as Northern Ireland's power-sharing executive sinks to its knees, the Prime Minister of the United Kingdom defends his decision to attend a one-day cricket international against Australia and visit Queen Elizabeth in Balmoral the following day. His defence is that he's never a yard away from his BlackBerry. Tony Blair stood on the steps of Stormont on 10 April 1998 and said it was not a day for sound bites and that he felt the hand of history on our shoulders. He really did. Now the hand of history has choked us to death. If this collapses, we are in real trouble. Nature abhors a vacuum, and I am sure that now the Assembly has been toppled, the men of violence will come out of the shadows and it will not be business as usual but violence as usual. It is just like my autism – there is no cure.

I now want to talk about my GCSE coursework. One of the tasks was to write about the community in *Of Mice and Men*. I find the title of that book so annoying – I mean, it's not even about mice. True, a mouse did have a cameo role at the beginning, a rather petted-to-death mouse which Lenny was hiding in his pocket and which George confiscated as it was starting to smell. The title is taken from a Robbie Burns' poem in which the speaker says, 'the best-laid schemes o' mice an' men | Gang aft agley, | An' lea'e us nought but grief an' pain, | For promised joy!'

Our teacher told us that the mice in the novel were a metaphor for human helplessness and ultimate destruction. The mouse dies, the puppy dies, Candy's dog dies, Curley's wife dies, and, in the last scene, Lennie dies. All of these deaths were accidents or mercy killings, as in the case of Candy's dog and Lennie. And the men, Lennie and George, represented the tragedy of the American Depression. In Steinbeck's novel there are 169 idioms, 155 examples of ambiguity, 134 metaphors and 23 similes.

The teacher gave us an example of a metaphor:

The curls, tiny little sausages, were spread on the hay behind her head, and her lips were parted.

And a simile:

Her hair hung in little rolled clusters, like sausages.

Now, to me, a sausage (and by the way I hate the smell of sausages, and when you think of the ingredients that go into making sausages it's enough to make you ill) is a cocktail of additives. I mean, do people realise that they are eating a concoction of sinew, soya, sulphites, polyphosphates, flavour enhancers and, yes, I believe there is some meat in there. I am not trying to make suggestions to John Steinbeck, but he should have used the term 'bangers' instead of 'sausages' for at least bang or bangs is a fringe of hair combed over the forehead. Although I did like this simile:

You're yella as a frog belly.

Colum Eastwood was speaking after the DUP MLA for Strangford, Michelle McIlveen, was today appointed to the post after being nominated by DUP leader Peter Robinson. She succeeds Ulster Unionist Danny Kennedy who resigned from the position following his party's withdrawal from the Executive. This cat and mouse game was introduced to disrupt Assembly business.

Colm Eastwood said, "The 10-minute ministers of the DUP are undermining these institutions, they are undermining the talks process and they're undermining the partnership between unionism and nationalism that should be at the heart of power sharing."

We have left fantasy budgets and zombie politics and are now entering nursery-rhyme land:

Oh, The grand old Duke of York,
He had ten thousand men;
He marched them up to the top of the hill,
And he marched them down again.

And when they were up, they were up,
And when they were down, they were down,
And when they were only half-way up,
They were neither up nor down.

Fearghal McKinney, SDLP, commented that, 'At least, the Grand Old Duke of York actually marched his men up the hill. The DUP might pretend differently, but it does not even know whether it is halfway up or halfway down.' Maeve McLaughlin said 'the situation has become farcical'.

Meanwhile I am going to have to find out if it would be better to resit my GCSE in November 2015 or if I should just repeat the whole year, not that I wouldn't relish helping to improve Steinbeck's metaphors. If I go back, I will fix Shakespeare as he left a few things unanswered. For example, what happened to Lady Macbeth's baby? She said:

> I have given suck, and know
> How tender 'tis to love the babe that milks me.
> I would, while it was smiling in my face,
> Have plucked my nipple from his boneless gums
> And dashed the brains out, had I so sworn as you
> Have done to this.

I will go tomorrow to the weird English teacher and more shall she speak, for 'now I am bent to know' what is the best thing for me to do. Now, what if our teacher decided to do a 'Duke of York' stunt?

> There was a grand teacher from Cork
> She had twenty-five students,
> She marched them into the class
> And then marched them out again.
> And when they were in, they were in,

And when they were out, they were out,
And when they were only halfway in
They were neither in nor out.

And come to think of it, what use are politicians? What can they actually do?

Can they bake a cake?
Can they make a milkshake?
Can they ice-skate?
Can they do an eye test?
Can they do a blood test?
Can they do an MRI scan?
Can they perform an appendectomy?
Can they perform a hysterectomy?
Can they write a memo?
Can they write a will?
Can they write a parking ticket?
Can they write a novel?
Can they write a poem?
Can they write a lesson plan?
Can they deliver a sermon?
Can they deliver a baby?
Can they baptise a baby?
Can they hear a confession?
Can they fight a war?
Can they fight a fire?
Can they give a flu jab?
Can they perform brain surgery?
Can they empty a bin?
Can they work at a checkout?
Can they pack groceries?
Can they arrange a care package?
Can they drive a taxi?

Can they taxi down a runway?
Can they complete a tax return?
Can they judge a case?
Can they paper a wall?
Can they paint a house?
Can they make a dress?
Can they play a role?
Can they roll a dice?
Can they play a saxophone?

Well, what can politicians do? They can do a lot of good things, for example they can bring in good policies and overturn bad ones. When a party comes into power they might see the country as a piano that need to be retuned or a beached whale that needs to be refloated or a vine that needs dressed. Now that the piano is out of tune, they can do good things. When the power-sharing Assembly took their seats in Stormont there was a sense of optimism, a sense that the politicians would not be weighed down by the burdens of the past. They were hailed as ambassadors for peace in the four corners of the earth, and they were asked to do international tours in order to speak about the miracle of transformation from guns to government. President Obama praised the peace process, Queen Elizabeth II applauded all those who had brokered the Agreement and pointed out that it gave hope to other areas embroiled in conflict. Former UN Secretary General Kofi Annan praised the way the politicians were able to reimagine their relationships.

> Now it has come to this. Now it's stasis.
> Trimble doesn't even want the US.
> Some are saying the UK doesn't want us.
> After all this sharing, there is no trust.
> Once it was the only show in town,
> Now it's breaking down.

Were you minister today?
Will you be minister tomorrow?
I am minister today.
But I will resign later this evening.

'Take some more tea,' the March Hare said to Alice, very earnestly.

A Storm in a Teacup (literally)

As talks continue today
About the Stormont crisis,
the Social Development Committee
has been discussing the important
issue of having free tea and coffee
at their Assembly meetings.
Stewart Dickson said:
'It might be helpful to
have a cup of tea or coffee
to commence the meeting.'
Jim Allister was against the proposal
As it would cost '£500 of taxpayers' money'.
Roy Beggs said: 'It's not the biggest problem
we face at the moment.'
Committee members voted in
favour of free beverages.
Mr Allister was the sole member who
voted against.
He may bring his own flask in protest.

As for me, I don't think I could be a politician. Our teacher told us that everyone born in 1998 was lucky. Lucky to have been born at same time the Troubles had ended. You know, I don't feel very lucky, and I don't think the Good Friday Agreement was very lucky either.

Friggatriskaidekaphobia

So Friday is not a very auspicious day. I know the Good Friday Agreement didn't fall on the 13th in 1998, but I still don't think it's a good idea to sign an agreement on a Friday. I mean, surely the 'good' in Good Friday is ironic, for after all on that day the Christian world commemorate the death of the son of God, an innocent man. What was good about that? After carrying out some research I was able to find out some of with the terrible things that happened on Fridays:

On Friday, 13 August 1521, Conquistador Cortés defeated the Aztecs. Montezuma II distrusted Cortés but feared him because he thought he was Quetzalcoatl, the Aztec God, and therefore sent him gifts of gold and chocolate.

On Friday, 13 November 1970, 300,000 people were killed when a monsoon flooded the Ganges River in Bangladesh.

At the same time there is research to suggest that thirteen is no more unlucky than any other number. The Italians think that seventeen is an unlucky number: in Roman numerals seventeen appears as XVII, and if that is written as VIXI it means 'I have lived', but this phrase could be a euphemism for 'I am dead'. In Asian cultures four is seen as a very unlucky number because it sounds like the word 'death'. The fear of the number four is known as tetraphobia.

I meant to say that I got an F grade in my comprehension. I ask you – who gets an F? I really thought I'd cracked that paper. And the funny thing is, the teacher had been explaining about headlines the very week before the examination. She had mentioned that one of the most famous opening lines ever was the first line in Herman Melville's *Moby Dick*, which is 'Call me Ishmael'. So I was thinking that if I got the chance, I would use a line like that. And then she revised CODFISH with us which stands for: Colour, Organisation, Diagrams, Font, Images, Slogans and Headings. These are the presentational features to look out for. Then you have to remember

AFOREST: Alliteration; Facts; Opinions; Repetition, Rhetorical Questions, Reader Focus, Reliable Source; Exaggeration, Emotive Language, Examples; Statistics, Shock Tactics, Structure; Threes.

The online article 'Killer shark off Cornwall? It must be summer!' was a gift when I opened the examination paper in June. I couldn't believe it! The colour image on the page in front of me was of a white shark in blue water – it was almost swimming towards me! I think our English teacher must be psychic because she had mentioned Melville's *Moby Dick* in the weeks previous. I really couldn't believe my luck – a marine theme! I was going to let these examiners know that I knew a thing or two about great white sharks. For example, their eyes are amazing: they have lenses, corneas and retinas, but their eyes also have a tissue called tapetum lucidum which helps them to see in the dark. I would let them know that the film *Jaws* demonises the great white shark. I mean, sharks don't hold grudges and they aren't monsters. They are no longer regarded as dangerous torpedoes with black, deadpan eyes but rather as charismatic creatures of the deep. Once a species gets scarce we view it as invaluable and slap a protection order on it.

I think Herman Melville was autistic, or at the very least he was on the spectrum. I mean, the chapter on cetology could only have been written by an autistic person. He wanted to present a systemisation of cetology; he decided the whale was a fish and called upon Job to support him. In book I, chapter I, he described the sperm whale as the 'spermaceti' that was valuable for its oil. Melville saw the sperm whale as the king of all the whales.

I liked the way Ishmael divided the whales into three primary books: the folio whale, the octavo whale and the duodecimo whale, and then he divided the books into chapters. He did this so that the reader could get an idea about a creature that no one had really come to terms with or categorised. For example, in chapter II, he describes the right whale, which should have been called the wrongly named whale because no one could agree a title for it. Was it called the 'Greenland Whale; the Black Whale; the Great Whale; The True Whale; the Right Whale'? Was it the 'Great Mysticetus of the English naturalists; the Greenland Whale of the English whaleman; the Baliene Ordinaire of the French whalemen; the Growlands Walfish of the Swedes'?

And in chapter III of book I the Fin-Back has been referred to as Tall-Spout and Long-John. And in the next three chapters he describes the Hump-Back, Razor-Back and Sulphur-Bottom.

Book II (Octavo) chapter I is based on the Grampus; chapter II, the Black Fish; chapter III, the Narwhale; chapter IV, the Thrasher; and, lastly, chapter V, the Killer.

In the third book, Duodecimo, he describes the smaller whales. Chapter I gives an account of the Huzza Porpoise, chapter II concerns the Algerine Porpoise and the third chapter is about the Mealy-mouthed Porpoise.

You will have to agree that Melville had an encyclopedic knowledge of whales and he was not afraid to write it down. He was writing in the good old days before writing coaches and critics stipulated that writers must 'show don't tell'; nobody can tell a dead author to write more succinctly.

Mrs Lundy, my English teacher, said that the question only wanted the student to list *four* things you learn about the shark reportedly seen in Cornwall, and to secondly write down what you understand about people's reactions to the sighting of the shark. I told her I couldn't resist the challenge when I saw that one of my favourite topics had turned up.

Well, as I draw my narrative to a close I am surprised that my failure in academia has been mirrored in the collapse of the institutions at Stormont. Someone said that we cannot even have a decent hurricane; we are an island at the edge of Europe, and by the time a hurricane gets to us it is a spent force.

If my career is going to resonate with the fortunes of the Assembly, I am flummoxed, to put it mildly. Surely a Good Friday's child should have a good innings and not be faced with sticky wickets and corridors of uncertainty? Surely a Good Friday's child's path should be littered with stardust not laced with fiascos. Surely a Good Friday's child should go from strength to strength not hand to mouth. Surely a Good Friday's child should have a Good Friday peace dividend not finish up at a dead end? It's like *Groundhog Day*:

> What would you do if you were stuck in one place and every day was exactly the same, and nothing that you did mattered?

The news is laden with snippets about the rows that have broken out since the DUP stepped down from their posts. People are asking, did they take their pay cheques or did they hand them back? People are saying that it's a disgrace that we have no health minister when people are languishing on waiting lists which are getting longer and people are living in pain and anguish.

The tomfooleries of the Assembly feels like *Groundhog Day* where Punxsutawney Phil meets Hamlet and maybe a little bit of Macbeth: 'To-morrow, and to-morrow, and to-morrow | Creeps in this petty pace from day to day.'

And now the new Independent Body will carry out another report, which will assess if any parliamentary activity still exists in the North. Just look at the murals and read the writing on the wall – the dogs on the street know what's going on, the rats in the sewer are savvy, the cows in the meadow know what's happening and the hens in the yard could give you a head's up.

Should we have a chequebook peace process? Should we invest in loyalist groups so we can help them move from militarisation to civic society? Should we invest in underachieving Protestant students? Can we throw money at the problem or is that throwing money away?

We could paper the walls with the Agreement documents. Do we need another independent body to monitor paramilitary activity? Does America need to get involved? Does Dublin need to get involved? Although a lot of water has flowed under the bridge, we still seem to be back at the same impasse. Can the ghosts from the past not be appeased? Do they have to be appeased before peace can be achieved or do we need more resignation? Can we never win at the roulette table or must we always cash in our chips and walk away? Has Peter Robinson stepped down or stepped aside or resigned? Is stepping down a euphemism for resigning?

We can't even deal with a flu epidemic, the health minister said. I do not like to end my manuscript on a downer, but I have no choice. The hand of history was upon me, upon us, as Blair said in 1998, and he said the burden of the past had been lifted. Looks like the burden of the past has descended upon us again and it's even heavier because we seem to have exhausted all the options.

I am not looking for a handout, just a hand-up. It is bad enough having autism, but living in a failed state compounds the problem. Can the politicians stop trying to score points and get on with the job they were appointed to do?

> And Samson took hold of the two middle pillars upon which the house stood.

Are they like Samson pulling down the Philistine's temple after he had been humiliated and blinded by them? Is there any point dismantling the Agreement after all the handiwork that built it? It may be flawed, it may be a diamond in the rough, it maybe needs a bit more polishing, and it certainly did not leave the architects unblemished, but it's better than returning to direct rule. It seems as if the children have fallen out and they have run to Mother to get it sorted out.

Some final thoughts.

> That this Assembly expresses concern over the waiting times for children for autism and special educational needs assessments.
> (6 October 2015)

I was disappointed with the motion over the delays in the diagnosis of autism in the province. Imagine, there are 1,300 children waiting to be diagnosed. Maybe I am lucky after all, for at least I was diagnosed. They use words like prevalence and arm's-length, collaboratively, streamline and protocols. It's all words to make them sound like they know it all, but, in reality, they are doing nothing at all. And I noticed that a lot of the benches were empty.

But, needless to say, they were not empty the day that the motion was raised to agree the Second Stage of the Special Advisers Amendment Bill – can you believe that? The bill was defeated. I now realise that although the DUP and Sinn Féin hate each other's guts, they are able to club together when it's an issue that means something to them. And can you believe what politicians earn – and that there are so many of them?

I suppose it's up to me to make the most of my life. I have autism, I was born with autism and there is no cure. I want to shout at the politicians and tell them to wise up and stop hiding behind jargon. What is protocol? The word is derived from Late Greek *prōtokollon*, which was the first sheet of the roll of papyrus and contained the date it was made. In Greek *protos* means first and *kolla* means glue. So what are the real protocols, prithee? What is the glue that is going to bind us together? Will Gary Hart, the US envoy, be the glue? Will we fly or fall? Will the Good Friday Agreement and the agreements that led up to it be trampled underfoot like Salman Rushdie's midnight children who were reduced to 'specks of voiceless dust'. Will the hand of history that Tony Blair felt be the hand that crushes me, grinds me like a piece of fennel to be scattered to the four winds?

There is always the chance that we can turn over a new leaf. We can make a fresh start, fresh start, fresh start, fresh start, fresh start, fresh start, fresh start, fresh start, fresh start, fresh start, fresh start, fresh start, fresh start, fresh start, fresh start, fresh start, fresh start.

Printed in Great Britain
by Amazon